A Prince of a Fellow

by Shelby Hearon

SHELBY HEARON

A Prince of a Fellow

DOUBLEDAY & COMPANY, INC.
GARDEN CITY, NEW YORK
1978

ISBN: 0-385-12538-0
Library of Congress Catalog Card Number 76–56298
Copyright © 1978 by Shelby Hearon
All Rights Reserved
Printed in the United States of America
First Edition

Library of Congress Cataloging in Publication Data

Hearon, Shelby, 1931–
A prince of a fellow.

I. Title.
PZ4.H4353Pr   [PS3558.E256]   813'.5'4

For Wendy and Sally

I cannot give you much.
I give you the images I know.
Lie still with me and watch.

Anne Sexton

A Prince of a Fellow

ONE

The Prince Appears

I am a frizzy-haired, washed-out princess looking for a prince. Some ordinary prince on a limping horse, to carry me off to his leaking, rented castle, to share his beans and salt pork and lie beside him in his bed. No one special; after all, I am nothing fancy. At thirty I have never established residence with a man, and those I have rubbed bellies with have been no better than I was willing to settle for. Concerned as I am with reality, I don't get my hopes too high; just a third son of a minor king.

Which search is the reason I had this morning in my radio station still another prospect, this one a writer down from Connecticut, here on a grant at the historic J. Frank Dobie Ranch. Which meant that for shelter he got an old farmhouse and for inspiration a field, a creek, and a view of the neighbor's cows.

I love to interview writers, as they are not fettered by facts. Thrusting characters and parrying plots spin from their fingers onto the yellow pad as slickly as spider webs. Silently inside their heads herds thunder and doors slam with a reverberation that we in the world of sound can only envy. Each time I coax a writer to open his vocal cords on my show I expect sudden magic; expect verbal rabbits snatched from the top hat of his subconscious.

Of course, I am habitually disappointed. Last year's Dobie Fellow, hungrily surfacing from under Los Angeles' thick sky, had spent six months staring through the barbwire fence at the milling livestock, his vocabulary locked in constipation. On the air, so full of his oneness with the land and its manure, he had had the opposite problem. I purposely omitted mention of his work in progress, lest it never progress.

I had high hopes that this year's visiting writer would be better. For one thing he possessed the irresistibly German name of Gruene Albrech; for another, his brooding voice, accepting my invitation to appear on my interview show, had suggested a prodigal son come home to confront an archetypal father—to kill or to forgive him (depending on the size of the Dobie grant).

Now, considering him through the pane of glass, he didn't look as I expected. He was not brooding at all; in fact, he seemed eager as a kid on his first day of school all decked out in new clothes, which he was—board-stiff jeans, creased Western pearl-snapped shirt, hand-tooled glossy leather boots. Even, sticking from his back pocket, a red bandana with the price tag still on it.

Right off I could see he was no German. Looking closer at his wide face whose skin stretched across high cheekbones tight as a drum, I decided he must be Slavic. His deep almost golden tan gave him a general yellow wash that appeared to color even the whites of his eyes and his teeth, and darkened to copper his bow-shaped mouth. In the manner of symmetrical faces, his chin was cleft in the center, Czech, there was no question.

That charade was all right with me; I was used to that. Things are seldom what they seem. None of us are as we present ourselves.

The old men in this fenced-in town in Central Texas, named for Prince Solms, the nobleman who brought their ancestors from the old country inland from the coast to this rolling edge of a ring of weathered hills, purport to live in a German-speaking hamlet.

In fact, they dream of a remembered past; today they make up less than half the town. Beer-bellied, polka-dancing Mexicans, heirs of the original land-grant holders, now outnumber the beer-bellied, polka-dancing German descendants of the prince's immigrants. Nor is this the lush verdant farmland they claim to their grandsons, hoping to keep them close at hand; only the thinnest veneer of grass and scrubby shrubs cover the rocky soil of this insular place whose factions shut themselves off from their neighbors as surely as its rivers cut apart its three hills.

We aren't what we claim either, here on my beloved Mole in the Tunnel. Our very show pretends one thing as it delivers another. KPAC, a remote broadcast station, sells itself as Pasture Radio, down home sound brought to you from the land of the Aberdeen Angus and Poland Chinas. Actually, although we pipe our audience the picking sounds of country and western's finest, we sit ten miles out of town on a rise so that we can beam our advertisers to the Porsche drivers and politicians in both San Antonio and Austin. We are no more authentically rural than Neiman-Marcus custom-cut bluejeans.

Otto, my sidekick, who gives the news and weather in heavy German accent, is really a forty-five-year-old Mexican, with Pancho Villa mustache, who works afternoons (out of his lederhosen and into his stiff black suit) as the cemetery sexton.

Nor am I, Avery Krause, the cowgirl my faded jeans and blue work shirts would imply. I am, rather, as my mama is, a Swede sitting like a burr in the saddle of a large German family. A corn on the sole of the old grandfather's foot.

For twenty years in the coal-burning state, as Papa in his German way called the black, gutted mountains of eastern Kentucky, Mama and I were mistaken for any other Appalachian towheads. Which angered Papa into deep silences over his journals and ledgers. I, so like the other schoolgirls with blue eyes pale as watercolor—all of us blanched, bleached, with peaked faces—made faint impression on the eye. We were Polaroid shots not yet developed. Now, come back here last year to bury Papa and replant ourselves, Mama and I are set apart from the Germans we married or were born into by our near-white curls, our wide thighs, even our sweet Swedish smiles.

If my appearance was the same in Kentucky, so was my

manner of dealing with the world. I was a drama teacher, which, if you think about it, is not too different from what I'm doing now. In both settings I present illusions as real. In both theater and radio the audience is let in on the hoax; together we share the thrill of belief suspended. Here, by consent, coconut shells pound into horses hoofs and squeaking doors signal mysterious entries and ominous departures. There, small white faces grew bold with greasepaint and eager hands slew dragons with broom handles.

So it was fine with me if today's prince was after all a golden impostor, faking his German birthright; I too make my living by delusion.

As I stared at his large dark head and wide palms which seemed designed to compensate for lack of height, he flashed a hesitant grin of greeting.

Wanting to get the feel of him before we went on the air, I put on the easy sounds of Willie Nelson's "Remember Me" and left the control booth to Otto, who was assembling the good tidings of local news and the usual bad tidings of local weather.

"Good morning, I'm Avery Krause. We talked on the phone."

"I'm here early." Gruene Albrech rose, short in the leg as I had perceived.

I shook his firm hand, deciding that the touch was worth coming out for. "Would you like a cup of coffee?"

"If it's no trouble. I left in a hurry. It looked farther on the map. I thought it would take me longer to get here."

"You were good to drive out at eight o'clock in the morning."

"I've never been on radio."

Which must explain the scrubbed look. People always forget we on radio see only with our movie-making minds.

"We're very informal," I tried to put him at his ease. "I'll ask a few questions, play some music. We'll let the listeners call in their comments. They like to feel they're taking part in the show."

Which in fact they did. The weekday interview hour was now the station's most popular feature, and the high point of Otto's and my shift. This was satisfying to me as last year, returned home and job hunting, I had sold KPAC's managers on the idea that visiting dignitaries and celebrities from San Antonio and Austin, and even stammering ordinary citizens from Prince Solms, telling their versions of daily events, would create a wider advertising market than followed their existing mix of country sounds, news, and weather.

"You can ask me about my book," the writer told me. "That's why I'm here."

I was more interested in him than in his proposed translation of himself into fiction, but, guessing he wanted a dress rehearsal, I asked, "What is your novel about?"

He cast about as if he hadn't thought of it before. "It's about these people."

Clearly he needed to warm up. Some writers obviously grew tongue-tied in the morning. Leaving his work, I moved to him, a matter of more concern to me anyway. "How long have you been away from Texas?"

He studied his cup. "Uh—since I left high school. Several years."

"Do you have family back here?" The Dobie grant as I recalled had to be bestowed on a native Texan.

"Uh—that's right. My mom's folks are from Vera-mendi."

"Czech?"

He looked relieved, as if the business of disguises bothered him. "How could you tell?"

"Long practice at observing dissembling."

"I guess I do that. Writing, I mean."

"Is Albrech your real name?"

"Actually it's Billy Wayne Williams." He looked sheepish at this admission.

"Why did you change it?"

"Who reads books by Billy Wayne Williams? If your name is Gruene Albrech they take you seriously. They give you a grant to the Dobie Ranch." He grinned. "They ask you to appear on radio shows."

"So they do." I smiled my blondest smile.

"Besides, I thought the German name would prepare me to tell my story."

"About these people—" I chided him.

"I'll tell about it when we're on the air. I don't want to waste myself now. I'm saving up for when it counts."

"Is that the way you write?"

"What?"

"Keeping it all inside until it goes down on paper?"

"I guess so. I never thought about it."

His crisp just-purchased clothes must also be a way to get into his tale and into this part of the country again. They did not look like the tweeds and Shetland sweaters I imagined for Connecticut. "How do you like being back here?" I asked.

"That's part of what we'll talk about." With that, he went back to the guest chair and turned his attention to waiting. Moving his knees apart and planting his feet squarely as a peasant, he simply sat.

It came to me I was observing an actor, off stage, getting into his role. A fine development, and one that I had missed.

Most people did not know that when the first sounds gave the cue that the curtain had gone up, we were on our invisible stage. Most people played to me, thinking me their audience. Most gestured to me, looked to me for confirmation, took my silent nods as answers. Most people did not believe that anyone was Out There; it would be grand to work with an actor again.

It took me back to another actor who had seemed, for a time, to be a prince of a fellow. An actor with a fine hairy belly against which I slept for five years of weekends. Remembering that earlier tale (or perhaps a later one) made me wonder about the writer before me—did he make love as the Czech rodeo rider or as the moody German?

However, I knew that such thinking was unproductive. After all, I had only taken one guest to bed, and he was no prince. Still, you had to consider it again each time; otherwise you ceased to take the risk that goes with looking.

Otto wrapped up his good tidings of local news with, "It vill be a goot day, as ve shall see." Popping his alpine suspenders, he plugged in a public service cartridge and signaled for me to take over.

"Pronounce my name *Green*." My guest spoke up suddenly. "That is the German way."

Then back in the booth the sorcery began again; we were crackling out over the air waves into the waiting ears. "Hello out there, this is Avery Krause on KPAC, Keep Peace, the station which brings you morning. Our guest today is that distinguished novelist Gruene Albrech, returned to the land of his forefathers in search of an ancient tale. You at home refill your freeze-dried and you in your economy cars move closer to your FM while we listen to his story. It isn't every day we get a real live word wizard on our show, so stay tuned and be sure to call in your own questions for him." At home in my eyeless world, I beamed myself to my unknown intimates.

"Tell us, Gruene, how does it feel to be back here in your homeland coming to terms with your past?" I fed him the cue.

With the first answer he was before the floodlights. His hands led him; his planted stance anchored him. He was Everyman, struggling to find himself and, in the process, each of us. As he talked he brushed his brown hair continually away, as if brushing aside deception or falsehood.

In the heavy tones of a Günter Grass he shared the anguish of going home again. He was the tortured expatriate, returned to wring the truth from the meager lives of his ancestors.

"And what is your novel about?"

"My book is a fable of a grandfather blinded by his villagers. It is a parable; for we are all that grandfather, the world is that village. Do you know the works of ——?" He plunged into a comparison of himself and a little known but powerful German writer, exiled from his home soil, writing of alienation.

Now I was not thinking of him in bed, but with his pencil and pad. Wondering if he wrote as this fine actor, the tormented Albrech, or as the golden cowboy. Most of all wondering did he write well?

"Do you write from your own experience?"

"I am everyone I invent, but they each transcend me."

"How do you know when your writing is good?" This was something I had never understood, as the actor is dependent on immediate response. The kids would put on a tablecloth, a bandit's cape, and ride their chairs backwards, and it was a good performance if their watchers shouted and clapped. And if they didn't, it wasn't. But for a writer the lapse from entrance to applause required a far vaster attention span to approval.

"Not until it's read. And then, if it comes from your deepest level of consciousness, you can only hope it will speak a truth to the deepest level of the reader."

He spoke then not of theater but of a message in a bottle, of himself stolidly gathering clams until the tide went out and came in again. Nodding my admiration of such patience, as well as such fine answers, I gave us both time to catch our breath and myself time to answer the blinking red phone that flashed a listener's call. Putting on John Prine's bittersweet ballad of "Donald and Lydia," I spoke into the off-air receiver. "Good morning, Keep Peace."

"How would you like to interview me tonight?" It was the all too familiar voice of the mayor of San Antonio. I felt a flush rise to my face. Wasn't it enough that I was still engaged in a shabby affair with this burgher in white socks; did he have to intrude himself into my ear as well on that ultimate invasion of privacy, the telephone?

"I can't talk now, Sterling, I have a guest."

He drew in his breath. It excited him to call when I was on the air, knowing he couldn't be heard by the audience but knowing it rattled me. He liked getting a reaction from me whenever it appealed to him—the usual attitude of a man to his mistress. "I can be at the cabin at a quarter to seven." Breathless, aroused by his call, he proffered the weekly rendezvous.

"How long will you have?" I did not relish the drive to our hideaway, a trip that took me more than an hour.

"I don't have to be at the reception until nine. Plenty of time for what I have in mind."

"I'll try to come."

"See that you do." He laughed, titillated by the double meaning. He knew I would appear; after a year it had become a foregone conclusion.

After a year he knew that he could count on my weekly treks to hear how things were going with his boys. He had surmised that whatever thrill the clandestine provided him, I was willing to settle for the feel of a man again.

As the music faded and Otto stroked his mustache in disapproval of the call, I invented a final question for our writer. "How long have you had this story in your mind?"

Through the pane of glass he acknowledged my invention, meeting my eyes above my flushed cheeks. "The blind old man surrounded by others," he concluded, "represents the primal scene in my life. I have never been without it."

If he writes badly, I admitted, I cannot bear it.

"Thank you for being with us, Gruene Albrech, and now stay tuned while Otto brings you news of the outside world from our fertile field among the mooing Angus."

Out in the front, I shook the writer's hand in thanks.

"Otto is Mexican, isn't he?" He studied the newscaster through the glass.

"His name is Ramirez. He's the cemetery sexton."

"He does a good imitation of the language."

"None of us is really German, are we?" I looked about the studio where we had each performed in costume. "Not to the grandfathers, anyway."

"I guess not." He looked away.

I studied his face, not knowing how to proceed. I had never known how to make overtures to men. If they wanted you then you either said yes or you said no, but it was their question before it was your answer. I had never learned how to move things along with the ones who didn't ask.

In Kentucky where I taught drama there had been a school principal who supported me in my attempts to get the mountain children to loosen their bodies, to wrestle a smile to the floor, or to pretend to be a caterpillar crawling in the dirt. He was one of those rumpled, dedicated men you always mean to end up with, conscientious and underpaid. Educated but with some flaw visible as a rip in his jacket which meant he had settled for a poor rural school in a backwater. In three years we never got past his encouragement and my redoubled efforts in the classroom. We never got past ending up at the same lunch table with our sacks of sandwiches and apples.

The one who finally did ask, the extravagant actor, had also, as Gruene had, rechristened himself. He had given himself, as he liked to pun, three *given* names. Called himself Charles Henry David in a take-off on the famous whose parents give them three surnames at birth (Custer Lincoln Grant). To his delight, people could never remember whether he was Charles David or David Charles. I called him Henry; I never knew his real name. At least this time, with the writer, I had got that far.

"Do you have time for another cup of coffee?" I asked, finally. "We could go watch the cows eat grass."

"Sure. I set the morning aside from my work."

We took our refills outside and leaned against the fence. There were no Angus in sight, nothing in the rolling green fields but air waves whispering messages.

"What did Billy Wayne do to eat in Connecticut?"

"How do you mean?"

"Nothing deep. English faculty?"

"Uh—yeah. The usual stuff. Teaching. Writers' workshops."

"Does Texas seem changed to you?"

"Everything stays pretty much the same down here."

I tried another tack. "When we were on the air, who were you talking to?"

He cast his eyes about, as if trying to visualize. "Just someone out there, I guess. Someone I don't know."

"I beam myself to a woman who is clearing the table, grabbing her things, getting into her sports car to go to work, taking me along with a fresh cup."

He considered. "I couldn't imagine anyone specific like that. If I did I would get involved in where he was going to work and what kind of car he had and then I would get into his wife and kids and their fights and that personal business and then I couldn't talk to him. I guess I was talking to the same person I write to: just someone out there."

"How long do you have at Dobie?"

"Six months. Isn't that standard?"

"Sometimes they give the grant for a year—"

"I figure if I can't get my book started in six months then I can't do it anyway."

"Do you write every day?"

"The research is what slows me down. I thought I knew my people but it is taking me longer than I planned."

It couldn't be going slower than my research on him. I could only guess that he had put on the new country clothes in order to leave behind the world of the teacher and method act his fictional villagers. "You made your tale very convincing to our listeners."

"I have never been on radio before."

Which was where we came in. Stymied, I watched as his hazel eyes focused on some scene out there past the fields.

Unexpectedly, he asked a sudden question of his own. "Who were you talking to?"

"I told you. Just a woman in her car—"

"I mean on the phone. When you made up that question for me."

"Oh." I felt the red come back again. "The mayor of San Antonio. A friend of mine." Which I guess spelled out the whole thing for him. But I didn't know what else to do but tell the truth; I did not bill myself as what I was not.

"You got opaque."

"How do you mean?"

"You closed up."

"I may do that a lot."

"That's not good for you."

I shrugged. Some things it was better not to stay open to. "It's self-defense."

"I know about that," he said.

"Around here you have to—" But he must remember all that.

"—Well," he said.

I asked one parting query. "Do you write in those clothes?"

"I never wore these before."

I didn't press further. Maybe he wrote in turtlenecks and corduroys, or, emulating the grandfather, in an old man's nightshirt. Maybe he got up every day and sharpened all the pencils in his cigar box, in the nude. Maybe I would never know.

We emptied our cups and scanned the horizon—toward Prince Solms and the lavender hills to the north, toward Veramendi and distant Mexico to the south. I had run out of inquiries. If not out of all I wanted to know, at least what it was possible to ask. Holding out my hand one last time, I called it a morning. "Thank you for coming. Otto will have to move onto ag news and polkas if I don't rescue him."

"Here—" He tugged the bandana from his back pocket and stuck it in my hand. "I don't need this."

I tried to leave things open. "Stop by on your way back to see the folks in Veramendi."

He left them closed. "Right now I'm working out the village in my head." Getting into a car as new as his name, his Levis, and his performance on my show, he backed out onto the unpaved access road.

I tied the bandana on my tow head. Sometimes you had to make do with souvenirs.

TWO

Re-enter a Toad

I stopped by Ybarra's grave on my way to see the mayor.
Here, in the land of the grandfathers, it is more help to
seek out the unknown and departed than the living and
kin.

Of the town's nine fenced plots, this one reserved for
Catholics who married outside the faith is my favorite. I
love its hope; daily prayers move the spirits of those still in
limbo and daily weeping waters each mound's garden of
gaudy plastic flowers set in Styrofoam. Its kneeling lambs,
risen angels, and tin crosses with their crucified tin Jesuses
all seemed to offer penance in the dusk.

Which is why I come: to be forgiven for sleeping with
the mayor of San Antonio, for making love where I do not.

Here in the world of the Germans which I was born into but will never be a part of, I felt from the start the need to admit to the shallow nature of my alliance with the mayor. I felt the need somewhere to admit that I was no better than I was. It seemed fitting to seek atonement here —among those whose very souls depend upon it.

A white cat dozed as usual in the pink cement niche that marked the remains of Vittoriamo Gutierrez Ybarra. Thirty-one artificial lilies shaded it from the slanting sun. The saintless painted grotto set with chipped blue tiles, the grubby blooms stuck as if rooted into the ground were all that remained of the grief of *sus inconsolables padres*, his inconsolable family.

Those, and my gift of Perpetual Care. Which means that Otto comes weekly, or monthly, to push away the cat, rake the dirt mound, and reset the dusk-streaked lilies.

I had met Otto at Papa's funeral, as, standing within the scalloped iron fence, each loop drooping with a metal weeping willow, he had guided the elderly black grave-diggers, giving them orders in his guttural accent.

"How come you speak the wrong language?" I had asked. (To distract myself; not wishing to attend to the wall of silence around Grandfather, not wishing to hear Mama's rising wail.)

"When I went to school the only second language offered was the German. So I had six years of it. At home we had only the Spanish. English I learned not so good from my German teachers. Now the government has changed things around and we have what is called bilingual education. So now the German sons take six years of the Spanish." Laughing silently, so as not to offend, he let me know he understood the joke, which was on all of them.

"What got you here, looking after the dead?"

"Same thing as you. A funeral." He told the story then of his mother, taking out a large white handkerchief to wipe his big face when the telling grew painful. She was a woman who had spent her life afraid of water. As a small girl a fortune teller had warned her that water was her fate. She would not swim. She sponged her body clean behind locked doors. She would not cross the bridged rivers of her life even for weddings. At each new infant's baptism she had to be carried from the church in fright. When she was thirty-seven a wall of water roared down the dry arroyo behind her adobe house. The flash flood hit her at the clothesline. "It was her fate," Otto explained.

This reasoned way my middle-aged co-worker looks at life is a truce his solid, trusting body has made with the world. If this was the way things were, then this was the way things were. Drawn to how Otto could admit the facts, I had adopted him as my first friend back home in this culture where the Germans sit in judgment on every act or its omission.

After my first time with the mayor I had sought the sexton out.

"How much would it cost, Otto, to tend a grave?" I had asked.

"Your father is cared for."

"Not him."

"One hundred dollars." His standard fee.

I led him past the pale remembrances and stone memorials of the German Protestants across the road through the highest gate into the plot of sweet excesses. "I want to care for this one."

"How come you picked him? From so many?"

"The white cat picked him first."

Otto had filled with pleasure at the gesture. "His wife can no longer come herself. She will think it a miracle."

"Why not let her think so?" We all exist on some mirage.

Behind the departed Ybarra, bleached wooden crosses marked four tiny infant spaces. Each promised: *descance in paz*, she rests in peace.

This buried borrowed family had become my kin in much the same way Pasture Radio had become my home: it was the preferable alternative. When you had only your dough-faced Swedish mama, trapped in the house of the bent and unforgiving grandfather, to turn to, then you looked elsewhere for comfort. Just as, when you lived alone in a temporary garage apartment, beneath the branching lagustrum, you gave your best energies to the place that took your word it was a good morning.

"Scram, kitty, time to get going." The dusty white cat stretched and wandered off into the sunshine. Rearranging the lilies into a clotted clump, I ambled off myself.

Some atonement made.

The absolute worst thing about the trip to the cabin is the anticipation, the dread in advance of inevitable fact, of the four kinds of ticks that inhabit its high grass, and, sometimes, its gravel pathway, and, always, its trees.

Stopped in the middle of the deserted country road, waiting for a herd of wild angora goats, barbarians from the hills, to move along, I could sense ticks clinging to the matted hair that swept the dirt.

The mayor had come into my life a year ago, amidst the raucous birds of February. I had interviewed him on KPAC; riding the public coattails had seemed a logical visibility-grabbing move and a good way to launch my new show. The Austin mayor, a bearded bore, had been my first interview; San Antonio's, my second. Arriving in white socks and Tyrolean hat, he looked an easy mark. Which shows that things are never what they seem.

He had brought with him a stack of typed cards from which he read his answers, irrespective of my questions. Repeatedly he interrupted me on the last word; consistently he stole my air. "I'm so glad you asked that, Avery, as it gives us an opportunity to repeat again what we feel to be one of the more pressing problems. . . ." Thumbing through his cards, he selected one from which to complete his comment. "As you must know"—he moved in smoothly mid-word in my query—"that is a serious situation to which we have continually given paramount attention. At this time we are striving . . ." Adroitly, he flipped another paragraph into his reply.

Not once did he even go through the motions of looking in my direction. He had mastered radio; at a time when I was still learning on the job, he had already grooved into his shopkeeper's head the essential facts of air and what it took to occupy it.

"Good job," I had conceded afterwards.

"Thank you. I'm pretty used to this by now."

"It's still new to me."

He had looked around the windowless box which is our studio and assumed the right to assess its possibilities. "You ought to have couple of easy chairs, over in that corner, for guests."

Instead, we had perched on the edge of the table that holds the visitor's mike.

"Your name can't really be Sterling Price," I told him. Having just come from a state which had no time for such jokes as Sterling Price or Ima Hogg. "Any day now I expect to meet someone back here named Furling Flag or Distant Drums."

Somewhat defensively, he had said, "They are both well-known Texas families, you know, Sterling and Price." Casting about for a light touch, he had added, "I used to date a girl named Cherry Stone."

Smiling at the trim man with his short stiff Kraut's haircut, I watched him calculate my potential as he had that of the studio. After a moment, unerringly, he pulled from his wallet pictures of his sons. "You want to see my boys?"

Sons. In this German world, here among the Krauses, the magic word, the magic fact. That without which you cannot enter the clan of the grandfathers. Papa, banished by a family feud to a grimy mountainside, remained all his life a failure. One wispy female child born to his Swedish hired girl of a wife could not elevate him to fatherhood in the Germans' eyes.

Sterling Price, with his bow tie and his military bearing, had known at once that one special thing he had to offer. With his politician's instinct had offered me his paternity, had known that in pulling out his sons for me he was revealing the one scrap of truth in his life.

"This is Clarence." He pointed to the elder. "He's a real achiever. An Eagle Scout at twelve, all that. This is Alfred. I guess you might say he's the black sheep. Not bad-looking boys, are they?"

"You must be proud of them."

"They give me a lot of headaches." Which meant the same thing.

"They take after their father." I admired the two tall kids standing stiffly in Sunday suits.

Pressing his advantage, he took my hand. Next week, he said, he would be in Prince Solms to address a meeting of *Die Ältern* (the elders). Checking his pocket calendar, he confirmed the date. "May I give you a call when I'm in town?"

"All right."

"On Tuesday, then."

The afternoon he called, I let him come to my apartment. There did not seem to be any need to beat around the bush. He was uneasy about parking his grand car where it could be seen from the street, and more so about going up my outside stairs, visible to any passer-by. In my cramped blue-walled space, he had reproached himself for incorrectly assessing the situation. "Next time we'll find a better place," he said. "I should have brought a bottle with me."

Our first undressing was not successful. I made the mistake—glad to be back in someone's bare arms again—of thinking of Charles Henry David the actor and his hairy belly. Immediately homesick, I could do nothing for either

23

of us. Sterling was distraught. "I know you girls like to take your time. I shouldn't have rushed. Next time we'll take it easy, you know, get relaxed."

The birds were the final straw. As we were dressing I heard what sounded like rain on the roof and then a great racket outside. It was not rain of course, not in Texas, in February. It was the robins come back to the lagustrum.

When we made our furtive descent down the stairs there was his car covered with purple bird droppings gummy as tar. Wild kamikaze pilots, the birds shot through the air above us, stripping the ripe berries, showering them like hailstones.

The mayor, in unaccustomed panic, suffered a painful loss of face. He was convinced that the entire Chamber, all his aides, and especially the wife would know what he had been up to by a single glance at the mess on his car.

While he composed himself, I hosed and scraped the sticky guano from the hood of his cream-colored Cadillac.

I had loved it all that afternoon of our maiden screw: his outrage, the swooping, squawking birds, the shit-on car. It seemed as fine a way to commemorate illicit sex as could be imagined. Besides, it had reassured me that things cannot always be correctly assessed; untoward acts can sometimes intervene.

Shortly thereafter, the mayor's weekend cabin was selected for our future rendezvous. High on an overgrown embankment, the cabin is on the wrong side of the Medina River; across from our ticks and goats are cypress trees and a clear swimming hole. The cabin is also on the wrong side of the mayor's life, dating from the days when his wife sipped a collins in her awful aqua and lime plastic place while he trudged down through the waist-high grass to take his beloved boys to play in the river. My theory is that young couples, as they were then, invested in such tacky leisure places so that, when they reached this later stage in life, they would have a mortgage-free spot to sneak to for their separate dalliances.

For the mayor, the cabin was a far better spot to meet than my apartment. It did not suit me as well. For one thing, I could never get through to him that whereas I had to make the long drive to San Antonio, circle it on the loop, pike up the interstate, and then crawl this tortuous road, he had only to speed along the artery from his downtown office to be virtually at its doorstep.

For another, the cabin had not provided me someone to sleep with.

Of all the things left behind in the coal-burning state—more even than the blurred yellows of merging dandelions and goldenrod—I missed someone in my bed. For five years of weekends, I had slept with Henry the actor. For five years, on weekends, whenever I rolled away in the night, he would reach out in drowsy reflex to pull me back against him, where I could feel the rise and fall of his breathing. Sometimes we slept spoon fashion, sometimes on our backs with our arms flung across one another, our legs wrapped around. Always we slept touching.

The first time Henry had appeared at my drama class, to entertain the kids, he was in top hat and white scarf trailing to his ankles. Wonderful, I had thought, a magician. And went home with him afterwards and straight to bed. Next time he appeared in a striped muscle shirt: a weight lifter. Grand. A quick-change artist. Then I had let him stay until Monday morning. One thing led to another, and to a trail of scarves, hats, wigs, cloaks around my rented room. And greasepaint stains on all my cotton sheets. It had been a lovely wealth of nights.

When the mayor first brought me to the cabin I had said, "I want to sleep with you."

We had made love once, and he was saving up to go slower the second time around. "Sweetheart!" He was delighted by what he took to be my eagerness. Consulting his watch, he explained, "It may take me a little minute to warm up the old motor again."

"Sleep, Sterling, spend the night."

"Oh." He looked surprised. "I'm afraid we couldn't arrange that here, too easy to track us. But, if that's what you want, I'll get us a hotel room in San Antonio. Soon, I promise. Here, you never know when the wife might . . ."

Our venture in said hotel turned out to be me locked for eighteen hours in one room with all-tile bath. Having lied about his plans to staff and spouse, Sterling spent most of the weekend checking the bolt on the door, hiding in the bathroom from room service, darting down the hall to the ice machine when the maids came to clean.

He had bought for me a brand-new black-lace nightie, for himself a soft porn magazine. Like any married couple, we read in our nightclothes, by the light of the color TV.

Like many, we slept in separate beds. After our last time around, he had handed me back my gown, put back on his green pajamas, and moved for the night into the other bed. "Don't be surprised if I come over and pull off your things in the middle of the night." Pleased to have it within arm's reach, should he want it, he had propped himself on two pillows and promptly fallen asleep.

In the morning, while he cleaned himself of me, I stood on the hotel balcony and watched lovers and tourists stroll on the winding walks below. Apparently, back here on home ground where rivers run past every door, you had to sleep alone.

Now, tired of the goats with their matted hair dragging the dust, I honked the horn and sent them stampeding up the rise, into a thicket of brush.

We had an unvarying ceremony in the lime and aqua hideaway. He greeted me with a kiss, after making sure my car and the cabin door were securely locked, then poured us both a shallow glass of scotch. A warm-up ritual.

Then we had a little talk about his city or his sons, before our first performance on the king-sized bed with its fringed spread.

"Hello, Sterling." I received the kiss by the car.

"I meant to get here early to get things ready, you know, air things out."

"I ran into the goats again."

"You have to honk."

"I do, after a while."

"Let me fix us a drink, sweetheart. Relax us a minute." He led me inside and secured us there, in the crowded unpleasant room in which a half dozen long ago hung and long since forgotten fish mobiles swung from the ceiling. Over a nonfunctioning fireplace a fisherman's net sagged at its cork corners. A room beached on its high, dry bank.

I had worn a pink clingy dress that he liked, whose

color, set against the bright green couch, reminded me of salt-water taffy.

Today Sterling matched, in a french-cuffed pink shirt. Usually unvarying in his merchant's white, he must have appeared on television; he had explained to me that you have to wear pastels to go before the camera's eye.

"What did you announce today?" I asked him, making small talk.

He touched his shirt front and beamed. "I just have to tell you things once, don't I? You really catch onto things in a hurry, don't you?" He reached over to pat my pink knee. "It was the kickoff for the upcoming prayer breakfasts."

"Prayer breakfasts?" A mayor's job included areas of concern unimaginable to the uninitiated.

"During Lent we plan to have one each day, down on the river, at outdoor tables. We're going to rotate the worship service among all the faiths and denominations."

"Who is we?"

"The City Council sponsors it, which is why I will be presiding. We expect tremendous crowds, since the breakfasts will be telecast and every congregation will want to have a big turnout. Today was the big publicity push."

"Who gets the important days?" I've learned that any detail I can imagine to inquire about, however seemingly small or irrelevant, will have already been the topic at several knotty city committee sessions.

As it had. "We had a lot of trouble with that. You can't believe how much in-fighting there is. If you'll pardon the blasphemy, they don't think God is invited unless their own church does the inviting. That's why we're taking turns. Everyone thinks it's always a matter of the Jewish, Catholic, and Protestant faiths, but you haven't seen anything until you see the Lutherans and the Baptists go at it."

"Who got Ash Wednesday?"

He sighed. "The Episcopalians. They're going to have *huevos rancheros*."

"It's good to get that settled early." I drained my drink.

"If this works out, at least we'll have some guidelines for next year."

"Obviously you've started an annual event to rival Easter morning." For fear of offending him, I had not said the resurrection.

Sterling reached for a breast beneath the silky dress. "I know an event I'd like to get started. You ready, sweetheart?"

Under the musty spread and permapress sheet, Sterling excited himself. Erotic scenes reeled behind his half closed eyes as he felt my small bosoms and thick white thighs. "Ummm," he murmured as his hands made movies.

Once his fantasy had taken hold he guided my head down beneath the covers until his manhood disappeared into my mouth. "Ahh," he spoke to images inside his head.

When it was my turn, I shook myself loose from memories of the actor's limber limbs and, retreating from the reality of the aqua-covered bed, let myself do the shopkeeper fantasy. . . .

He was a storeowner, in short sleeves, cuffed pants, white socks. He was fidgeting with his shelves and inventory. I was a rich customer in high heels and silk shirt. Finding us alone in the store, I unbuttoned my blouse and showed him my round doughnut breasts with their big brown nipples. When he came over to me, blinking and puffing, I reached a hand down into his pants. In a despair of desire he rushed me behind the curtain of his storeroom, where, removing my underpants, he pressed it into me on top of a packing box, bringing me as the door chimes sounded the arrival of a customer.

Warmed enough for mounting, I let the weight of the mayor ride my accomplice's body, as, all the while, against my instep, one white sock kept time.

"Was it all right, sweetheart?" Returned to the pale form beneath him, Sterling stroked my damp frizzy hair.

"Fine." My face was turned away, lest I see myself lie.

"Let me fix us another drink. Loosen us up a bit."

Back in the living room I sat with a towel wrapped around me, rolling scotch down my throat. My legs (like Mama's, heavy at the top, descending to fragile ankles) stretched out to reach the lime-green coffee table. "What are your boys up to, Sterling?"

"I don't know what we're going to do about Alfred." He was in his undershorts and open shirt. His face, which usually kept itself in a camera-conscious smile of composure, sagged with my tugging reminder of his fatherness. "He got three unsatisfactory citations from his teachers, you know those mid-term progress reports they send out. I don't know what to do with that boy. His mother and I have run the gamut of solutions."

"How is Clarence?"

"No doubt about it, that boy's going to go far. He's got my daddy's drive. Did I tell you he was a merit semifinalist?"

As a matter of fact he had, once a week for a month. Before that he had filled me in on the taking of the anxiety-making college entrance tests; on how his son, the good student, had prepared for them, on how much rested on their outcome. I reminded him, "You were proud of that."

"I did tell you, didn't I? I guess I'm still impressed with his scores. There's no stopping that eldest kid of mine."

What I loved most about his talk of his sons was that Alfred, the black sheep, was so clearly his father's favorite. At the mention of his name a dampness always came to his eyes and a softening to his cheeks. It was as if, for the length of time we talked, he was able to do what he had never been allowed to growing up: try on the feeling of a willful boy, a recalcitrant son.

"Alfred will be all right," I assured him, as I always did.

"You think so?"

"I know it. He's just sowing his oats, getting even with Clarence. It's hard to follow the oldest child, remember?"

"That's true. When I came along my brother had already—" He let his voice trail off, unhappy with the curtain he had raised on bad memories. "You getting relaxed?" He scooted over beside me.

"Do you have time?"

"We'll make time." He undid the towel and needfully pressed his face against what he found. This was safe ground. He knew how to deal with this. "Ummm," he whispered, coming up for a kiss. "What do you say we try again?"

My chore, while he showered behind the lime and aqua plastic curtain, was to remove all traces of our visit—wash and dry the glasses, make the bed, plump up the couch. I was not allowed a shower as that might leave behind one fair, incriminating pubic hair for the wife to find.

Toweling dry, Sterling launched into plans for next time. He did not like the little death of leave-taking. He preferred to think himself not departing this week's bed, but heading toward next week's embrace. Tucking the limp part of himself (which had not vanished but merely slumbered) into his trousers, he made promises. "I can make it earlier next week; you won't have to drive back in the night."

"That would be nice."

By the time he had installed me in my car and roared off ahead, it was dark down even into the grasses. Out on the narrow road I stopped to eat my supper sandwich, as crumbs were not permitted in the cabin. Massed in the middle of the dirt trail before me, the shaggy, dragging goatherd was like some collective woolly mammoth. A throwback to an earlier era—as was my affair with the mayor of San Antonio.

THREE

At Grandfather's House

Each Sunday before the noon meal with Mama and Grandfather I lay in bed and worked out the boundaries of my self.

As a small child in the shadows of the coal-hollowed mountains, I used to do this while the grownups slept. It was an effort then, as it is now, to discern where the world left off and I began. Facts were subject to construction. Fingers that felt other things were themselves a part of you but what they felt was not. Eyes that saw were in your head but what the reflections (which were also in your head) reflected were not. Sounds came to rest in the chambers of your skull, echoed there, died there, but the noise was not, at least at the start, a part of you, not until you had taken it in. What you read was not you, but then, after you had read it, it was you. All of these things became you, as food did, when they were put within.

At least that is how it seemed then. I am, fortunately, no longer so simplistic—thank God everything that goes in you doesn't become you, not to mention the mayor of San Antonio by name—yet now, grown, I still retain the feel of those confusions; still believe that all women must have trouble knowing what is them and what is not them. Not just the obvious that when you are penetrated he is in you but is not of you, but other ways as well. When you bleed the blood is you, but then, as it comes out, it is not you. It must be the same when milk comes from your breast to feed an infant; it must be you as it emerges from you, and yet it has been called forth by another, has not been in you in all the previous years that you were you. The egg in you each month is you, and yet your ovarian secretions function for its benefit as opposed to yours, so that even your own body does not comprehend what is it and what is not it.

When a woman carries a baby it is in her, but it is not her. Or is it? Was I Mama when I was in her? If so, when did I become not her? When I quickened? When I was born? This Sunday noon at her dinner table?

I have separate trouble distinguishing my connection with Mama and my difference from her. By the Germans we married into or were born into we are lumped together, as if two kolache or two dumplings or two rising loaves of Swedish bread. Yet to me, it is crucial that we not end up the same. I am haunted by a photograph of her which stands in a gold frame on Grandfather's mantel. She is a radiant young girl clinging to the arm of a narrow-shoul-dered boy who looks like Papa. She wears my same frizzled hair and light eager eyes. She leans against him with my thin arm and flaring thigh. Preparing to live happily ever after, she, Olga Dolle, the bride, beams out at all of us.

Now, in the bulging tiptoeing woman at Grandfather's house I can find no resemblance. When did that slim ex-pectant girl become this obese, cowed woman? When she took the German's name in matrimony? When she labored sweating all through the night to make them one six-pound girl? Or was it all those summers in Kentucky when she didn't make a son for Papa? When, each spring, she would swell up, a risen cake with her new pregnancy, and then, each sticky hot sooty midsummer, sink back, a fallen one; her latest heir flushed away with the rest.

If I have no answers, I retain much ambiguity about the transformation of Mama through her half-baked babies. For one thing they have left me with confusion concerning what is known as family constellation. On imaginary biog-raphies, I always list myself as the eldest of many. Al-though in theory, as an only child, I should have felt each time a vaster, less plural self, in reality each year I failed to become an older sister, there was less of me. Inversely, with each attempt of Mama's white flesh to reproduce it-self again, she ballooned into more of her.

Unsettled by a fear of repeating whatever steps turned her from her earlier to her present self, I have avoided those entanglements that could lead from a cheek pressed against a hairy belly to those miscarried infants, that enormous bulk, or the fading of the light in those expectant eyes. I flee down goat-packed back roads to the stagnant safety of those already married.

This morning I touched base with such distant limits of my self as nose and toes to gather within identifiable boundaries some general sense of *Avery*. And arose—to Grape-Nuts, skim milk, and the paper. On Sundays my blue-walled garage apartment does not seem a rented way station, but a home. That is because on Sundays the alternative is not Pasture Radio, but dinner at Grandfather's.

We ate in the room whose faded tablecloth, vacant fireplace, and dusty curtains were all that remained of the bustling dining room where once Grandmother Magdelena snapped green beans for supper.

When Mama returned here to settle, as if it were the natural thing to do, she moved back in with the grandfather, acting out the role of a widow woman silently seeing to the household rituals of stirring and wiping. Given the small room which had once been Papa's, and, later, mine, she took over the chores of any Swedish maid with scrubbed knuckles and white hose.

This noon, as every week, Mama fed us a tardy meal of greasy dumplings, tough chicken, lumpy potato soup, and cold light bread. By the time we had our blessing, the ice had melted in the tea glasses. Grandfather, the setter asleep against his feet, sighed and applied himself.

Grandfather had never meant to end up a son-less old man. His ancestors had made the long voyage from the old country to the Texas coast; had survived the grueling inland trip past Comanches, wolves, and vultures to a rocky scrub-oak farm in the hill country. Grandfather was the first generation of his family to come into town to school; his was the first to learn the new language. "You will have the college," his mother had insisted. "Today you must have the college." If he was the first to speak English in his home, he was the last to speak German in it as well. This diluting of the ways of the past was enough misfortune for a man to bear, but to be with brittle bones and have no grandson as well was enough to make a lesser man tap his cane and curse his God. And all the doings of the Swedish girl who now fed him grease-soaked dumplings and store-bought bread.

This house had been different in Grandmother's day. When Magdelena was in command there were no idle hands to tempt the devil. Each afternoon she set the copper kettle to boiling with lye soap, in which she dunked and twisted and wrung out the brine-soaked shirts and BVDs of the men who spent the day making fodder in the fields. Each afternoon she wrung the necks of the great fat hens that were to cook down and simmer with the dumplings for the heavy meal which was the nightly due of Grandfather and the uncles and brother who worked the land with him. She stoked the wood-burning cook stove and carried buckets of water from the well to boil the vegetables and scald the corn meal. Dinner was a groaning board of hens, succotash, garden greens, hot breads, and floating custards. On the Sabbath the men wore stiff white shirts and neckties to her table.

When Grandmother was alive I looked to her for the truth. Not given to the ingrained silences of Grandfather or the new ones of Mama, she kept her quick tongue going whenever there were things to be commented upon. "Mind me, Avery," she would say, "nothing good will come of such ideas." Or, rocking back and forth on the front porch, snapping or scraping or slicing, she would lean her solid face toward mine, breathing certainty along with dentures, and confide, "Men do not have to know everything that goes on under a roof."

I missed that sorely, the truthtelling, here in this sparsely settled house where everyone kept secrets and bore grudges.

This house was also different when Papa lived here. Then, already stooped and pinched by the time of my earliest memories, by the strain of kinship and his columns of close figures, he nonetheless used his clever hands to pull me as best he could into the clan. "We Krauses have been here as long as the state of Texas," he would brag over his Saturday afternoon ale, setting me on his lap so his papa would have to deal with the fact that I existed. "The Krause women you know can always have their pick of men," he would remind his mama, flattering her, but at the same time putting me and my skimpy blondness in the same class.

Sometimes, when Grandfather was slurping his gravy and Mama was slathering butter on her thick slices of bread, I could see Papa round the corner from the hall with a rare and cautious smile at finding me waiting for him. "You're as good as anybody, don't forget," he would tell me, twisting my tangled curls with his agile fingers. Although most of the time I suspected he told himself that rather than me.

Once, almost my only memory of our being alone, he took me out to the cemetery, in a pickup truck that belonged to Grandfather's brother. He had promised to deliver something from the uncle to his father and, out of his cubbyhole office, had decided to take me along. On his sandy frame his mother's bustling hands and his father's dour visage coexisted. Yet despite the tight lips and the muscle that jumped continually in his jaw, he had one of those appealing, always slightly hoping faces—I thought him a very handsome man, although probably he wasn't.

"This is where I brought your mother to propose. In those days I was sort of tongue-tied. 'I want you to be buried with my people, Dolly,' I told her. And she giggled the way she does and said, 'Whatever do you mean, Gus?' It was my way of offering her all I had, my family. Well, that didn't take. By now it looks as if she was vaccinated against them. But that doesn't have to hold true for you. You don't have to forget that you belong here. They may not have had much to say in life, and they certainly are a closemouthed bunch in death, but they're the best stock around these parts. Don't sell yourself short, when it comes time to marry. I can vouch a person can get into a lot of trouble that way."

Now, Grandfather, his plate cleared, begged out of the gummy pudding that was dessert. "Thank you for the fine meal, Dolly, I'll just have my coffee, if you please." This was his custom; to stir his noontime cup into a tepid milky sweetness, then, muttering his thanks, to slip out the back door and walk his dog Rufus across the fallow field. "Avery, if you'll excuse an old man, please." His eye on the door, Grandfather gave his dog a nudge and started to his feet.

Usually Mama, offended, kept her own countenance. If

he had on his mind better days when he had a wife who knew how to fix a proper dinner, she had on hers remembrance of her Gus who would reach across to pat her in thanks for any meal she served.

"Not yet, Gustav," she told him, a fat white woman in sprigged housedress and tight corkscrew curls. Her whole bulk moved forward with the resolve of raising her voice to him. If her chins were too creased and her arms and legs too marbled for rapid motion, and her squinting watery blue eyes too timid to flash resistance, high on the yeasty mass of her cheeks a brilliant spot of color gave away the effort of defiance.

Grandfather sat back down. He had not expected this, and therefore had prepared no resistance to it. From long habit, he gathered his outsized features into general disapproval. A meager-sized man, he seemed all face: jutting brows, protuberant nose, thick, raised, moist lips enclosed by hanging jowls the color of cold boiled potatoes. His coarse features, when set in opposition as they were now, made even his mildest reply a rebuke. "Can't it wait, Dolly?"

"Not this time,"

"What, then?"

"I'll not have Gus lie next to that man."

Grandfather, guessing her meaning ahead of me, implored, "Please, Dolly, that is water over the dam."

Mama turned to me, the witness for which this scene had been arranged. "The uncle is dying, Avery, and I'll not have him laid beside my Gus. They did not speak in this life; they'll not lie together in the next." Under the table her tiny white shoes drummed the floor.

Grandfather exhaled a large impatient sigh. "The church feud was a long while ago, Dolly. Let it lie."

"Some of us haven't forgotten it."

None of us had, of course, not even I, as it was our reason for packing up and leaving Prince Solms. "You can keep your books as well in the mountains as here, Gus," Mama had told Papa. "I have kinfolk there who know how to stick up for their own. I'll not stay in this town to be looked down upon."

Grandfather had not forgotten the feud either, although it was not the Germans' way to speak of past unpleasantness. Twenty years ago a splinter faction in the Reform Church had raised the question of English-speaking Sunday services. To the grandfathers this was heretical; if the church also ceased to honor the language then it would be forever gone. Was it not enough, they had muttered, that the young had grown lazy and careless, and insolent to their elders; must they now also allow the congregation to be overrun with yellow-haired Swedes who could not understand what was said from the pulpit?

For twelve months the Germans talked of this behind closed doors, but their secrecy had been in vain; a schism occurred and a vote was forced. The shame of making public their dissension had to be endured. Arrayed against the guardians of the language were the young, the new to town, those who had married outsiders—and the populous dough-faced Dolles. The grandfathers, who had fled to this country to build this very Reform Church, were defeated by two votes.

The uncle, Grandfather's brother and the father of five sons, had counted the ballots. When his side lost he had decided in his unforgiving mind that the two votes which had killed his church were those of his nephew and his nephew's Swedish wife. The blood tie, that closest of all bonds between men, had been severed. He never spoke to young Gus again. "Water is thicker than blood when it is Holy Water," he was heard to say. Although he still played cribbage and dominoes with Grandfather once a week at the lodge, the uncle's heart had hardened. He did not come to the station when the son left with his wife and ten-year-old daughter for the shafted slopes of Kentucky; when Olga returned with her husband in a box, the uncle did not come to the funeral.

At Papa's graveside, Grandfather had leaned on his cane, still as a stone, heavy as a weight, watching his last hope for the future go down into the sod.

"Let sleeping dogs lie," he told Mama now. "My brother is a dying man. What harm can he do?"

Mama had not been allowed to mourn Papa the way her people did. Seeing him go down into the yawning dirt, one of a row of ten ivy-covered, concrete-encircled Krauses, she had screamed, "Gus, oh, Gus," until her German in-laws stuffed a handkerchief into her wet mouth to still her cries. Had clung to the casket until they pried her loose. For this she had not forgiven them. "I have not forgotten, Gustav. I'm going to dig Gus up and put him with the Dolles. Let everyone see where he belongs. My ways are not your ways, Gustav. I don't mind saying in public who is to blame."

"I entreat you, Dolly. Don't commit an outrage against an old man."

"My mind is set." Mama began to clear the pudding cups, as if it were any Sunday meal.

Grandfather turned to me, hoping for a placating word.

"It isn't my doing, Grandpa," I evaded, not wanting to be caught between them.

Stiffly he got up. "Rufus and I will take our walk." Slowly he wrapped his thick lips about his pipe before opening the back door and leaning his aging bones into the first gusty winds of March.

"I have the money for it," Mama told his retreating back, touching a secret pouch beneath her ballooning dress.

In the silence of her victory, she sat back down, chins quivering, aimlessly finishing Grandfather's uneaten dessert. Picking the raisins out with her dainty fingers, she said, "They will see that I am set on it."

"You caught him by surprise."

"That is the only way." Firmly, she seized my arm. "Tell me how do I get them to do it, at the graveyard?"

"We'll go see Otto, the sexton. He'll know."

"I have the money, tell him."

"You can tell him. I'll drive you out there. It's a lovely afternoon to see the cemeteries."

"That's not natural." She sniffed, offended. "I must do up the dishes first. Gustav will expect it."

As I drove her to see Otto, I mused that in Prince Solms you could always tell exactly who and where you were. The town's living, separated by two rivers, were as divided as its dead fenced in their plots. My theory was that the early immigrants who had followed Prince Solms-Braunfels and his nobles to these promised acres had felt at once at home with the land's natural segregation.

We drove down the winding streets of River Hill, site of the stone fortresses from which the first German government had repulsed the Indians. This high land, looking out toward the hill country's weathered remains of ancient mountains, now belonged exclusively to the grandfathers.

At its base, we crossed the transparent spring-fed Weser River and climbed the steep slope of Corn Hill, on whose wide bluffs bloomed the nine flower-weeded cemeteries. On this broad-backed hill coexisted descendants of the earliest German settlers, heirs of the few blacks who had toiled alongside them, and those Mexicans who claimed lineage from the owners of the original land grants. Thus Corn Hill—which belonged to everyone, and therefore to no one—formed a natural buffer between the bulk of the Germans on one side of the clear Weser and the mass of Mexicans across the crashing commercial rapids of the Hidalgo River to the east, on Mill Hill. This large, tightly knit community of Spanish-speaking families filled more than half of Prince Solms's schools and supplied more than half its labor force. Isolated by language and custom from the isolating language and customs of the Germans, these families, such as Otto's, clung to the ways of their ancestors.

Each river-divided group laid claim to being Prince Solms's oldest inhabitants. To those Germans whose kin had routed the Indians to stake out a town, the late-arriving, border Mexicans were immigrants; to the landed Mexicans whose forebears had occupied the area since Texas was under Mexico's rule, the scruffy Germans were immigrants of the poorest sort. To both, the Swedes and blacks had been categorized a necessary work force. In recent years all of these groups could fling the hated epithet at those ragtag, no-nationality laborers who swarmed periodically into town to work the revenue-producing cotton mill—and breathe its powdered fibers, and live in shacks under its shadows, and wade its waste-water creek.

Predictably, as we passed Corn Hill's double square and caught sight of the roaring Hidalgo, and across it the mill, Mama leaned on her scant credentials. "Those immigrants live just like pigs."

I parked and went in the sexton's cottage, leaving Mama to wait for help by the car.

Otto, pleased to see me in the doorway, asked, "Who did you come to visit today?"

"Mama's with me. Come to bury Papa."

Putting aside his plot records, my heavy friend in his black suit stood up and stroked his mustache. "We did that already."

"In the wrong place, it seems. He isn't to stay with the Germans."

Frowning, he followed me out the screen door. "Good day, Mrs. Krause. How are you?"

Mama turned to me, to explain.

"We want to move Papa from the Krauses' to the Dolles' plot."

Without blinking, Otto named his standard fee. "It will be a hundred dollars."

Below her sausage curls, Mama's thin brows shot up.

Was she to pay now? "I have the money." She clasped the bulge beneath her flowered dress.

"Not yet, Mama."

Gently Otto approached her, making the hint of a bow. "There is one question to consider, ma'am. Will you want to retain the ivy of the present grave or go with the sea shells of your family?"

Holding onto her hidden wealth, Mama waited for him to get to the heart of the matter.

He coughed lightly. "At today's prices, ma'am, to locate the sea shells and set them in cement would be expensive."

Up and down bounced Mama's head as a stream of words poured fourth. There was no question about the matter. The son would keep the Krauses' ivy. Let anyone who drove by see that buried among the shell-encrusted Swedish mounds was a German whose own family had said that water was thicker than blood.

"If you'll walk this way with me, ma'am, we can select the lot." Gingerly Otto propelled her down a wide gravel drive.

"Avery?" Mama called to me.

"You go on. I'll wait for you here."

As she followed after him, her tiny feet selecting resting places for her enormous legs, I heard him say, "Have you settled on a day to move your husband's casket?"

"You'll hear from me when Uncle is still warm in the embalmer's hands."

"Yes, ma'am."

I walked past Papa's present grave, thinking of his pride at lying with the Krauses, thinking of his visit here to the one place he felt he could claim his kin. I preferred to leave him, in my mind, walking in the field of goldenrod behind our first Kentucky home, the trailer house. There he had existed, if discontented and wishing himself the whole time home, on his own two feet, and not as a descendant of the Germans.

Instead, I wandered on to Grandmother Magdelena's grave, also enclosed within the iron weeping willows. Beneath an arch of stone, carved with bending stone roses, she, as all the Krauses, had been sodded down by the Reform Church's two elderly blacks—tired workers with cloudy eyes who no longer remembered how they had first become the "old nigras" who retained the back-bending task of interring the departed.

We were not here for her funeral, and I was unable to envision it without her standing there, giving instructions to the laboring men, as well as to all her survivors, especially to Grandfather, who had never prepared himself for getting on alone without his wrung-out hens and shirts.

Sitting on the concrete oval which enclosed her leafing ivy, I traced with my finger the carved didactic rhyme above her head. Reading:

> Je schneller ich von euch gewichern,
> Je näher bin ich nun bei Gott.
> Mein korper, welcher ganz verblinchen,
> Der schläfet nur, und ist nicht tot.
> Gott hat mir Sicherheit verschafft,
> Und mich von ungluck weggerafft.

I translated as best I remembered from Otto's words:

The faster I have moved from you
The sooner am I now with God.
My body having withered quite
Is sleeping just.
God did procure with safety me;
Has torn before the evil me.

It was just as well she had lidded her eyes some fifteen years ago. This new sin against kinship, this moving a son from his designated resting place beside his uncle, would have been an unpardonable cold stone against her heart, would have been the final faithless act of the Swedish white trash.

Nothing but shame, in Grandmother's eyes, had followed the son's taking Olga Dolle to wife: the feud, the leaving, the unfruitful pregnancies following. Even the feckless and inappropriate naming of her only grandchild.

A version of that fury came back to me. Grandmother was in her bedroom, taking down her hair, removing the tortoise pins and letting the heavy tresses, cinnamon in their length, gray at the crown, fall to her waist. Proud of her good shape in her corset and ruffled shimmy, she told me, "I was a fine woman in my day. A decent son's wife would have called you after me. There'd have been no shame in that." In anger she slammed down the silver-handled brush on the dresser. "Who knows where she got such a name. It's not decent for a granddaughter of mine."

Back at the car, Otto patiently returned Mama to my care. Her plump hand tugged at my arm as she whispered, "Ask him how do we hire the old nigras?"

"We can do that later, Mama."

On my way out of the winding maze of monuments and fences, I parked on a side road between the German Catholics of the cemetery of the Blessed Saints and my friends in purgatory. As long as I was here, in the sunshine, on the Sabbath, why not pay my respects to Ybarra? If I regularly atoned for simulating love where I did not, how much greater the need for penance now when I raised no hand to halt the uprooting of him that I had loved.

"Why are you stopping here?" Mama peered out the window in dismay.

"You need to catch your breath before we go back. This has been a hard day for you, Mama. Look, I brought you some sugar cookies. You sit here and eat."

"It's not natural," Mama protested, reaching for a sweet.

But I was already ankle deep in purple thistles, savoring the whipping wind, the lambs, the wreaths, the rows of nailed-on crosses, thinking: Sunday with the family only happens once a week.

FOUR

The Woman with the Cut-glass Eyes

Otto had come to the studio in his black sexton's suit with his hair parted in the middle and his mustache neatly brushed. After the show he had official business down the road: dead to bury at Memorial Gardens.

"Want to see a Masonic funeral?" He invited me along.

Memorial Gardens was the new fashionable place to lay your loved one's last remains. A vast perpetual-care cemetery, a field of flat brass name plates embedded in grass, each marked by a durable urn of nonfade flowers. How could you mourn your dead when there was no painted cross or eyeless grotto to cling to? Not there. I tell him so.

"You complain that everyone in Prince Solms is fenced

in. Come see how you like a graveyard with no fences, not even around the families."

" 'In Flanders fields the poppies blow . . .' "

"There are not even crosses at Memorial."

"Who died?"

"A Mason, like I told you."

"Will they mind if I come along?"

"They will think you are one of his friends."

"What if they think I'm his girl?"

Otto burst into a laugh. "They would know that. His friends."

"What about his wife?"

"She will be grieving for him."

"I'd love to see a cemetery with no fences, Otto."

After we closed the show, we climbed into his elderly well-mannered Chevy and started out the stretch of road that separated Prince Solms, settled by the Evangelical and Reform Church, from Veramendi, a town of almost identical size and composition, which was settled by early German Lutherans—now largely Czech, as Prince Solms is Mexican.

Reminded, Otto asked, "Have you heard from your Tex-Czech?"

"Billy Wayne? No."

"They move slow."

"He may not move at all."

"After a while he will."

"How can you be sure?"

"His mind was on his story when he came. It will take a while to get it off."

Otto and I had talked, when we first began to work together, about the fact that neither of us had married. "How come, Otto?" I had asked him. "I see you out with women at the dances and festivals. They all look willing."

"Most of them are," he had admitted. "It is not my fate. You get a wife and then you get the children and you end up in a different place. The truth is, you end up in the same place you started out. I don't mind living on Mill Hill; my brothers are all there also. But if I want to leave it, I can. They can't do it."

"Maybe it's my fate, too?"

"It will be if you hang around his honor, your mayor."

Now I asked, "How can you tell a prince when you see one?"

"Don't rush him," Otto said. "They don't move fast."

The drive was away from the hills, toward the flat rich farmland to the south. Already the roadsides were bursting with flowering crab apple and pear; farmyards bloomed with hollyhock and red and yellow zinnias. Mama would love such homes. We passed a flock of white Leghorn hens, their hundred wings flapping like laundry in the wind.

"How would you like a woman to give the club news on our show?" Otto glanced at me slyly.

"Not much. If it's news it ought to be news whether it has to do with women or men."

"What if she was Queen Esther from the Missionary Baptist Church who was also on the national boards of seven charitable organizations?"

"In Prince Solms?"

"She is big in philanthropies. She has an eastern accent."

"How did you find her?" With delight I imagined the

deception of a vast black clubwoman in crepe dress with jeweled brooch, reporting in cultured tones on the German women's raffles, rummages, and bake sales.

"She is a sister to one of the old gravediggers. When I heard her talk with him, I thought of it." Otto had stretched himself in the year we had worked together to see that although things were the way they were, sometimes you could fool people with them. He was a child who had learned to hide behind his hands and make you think he'd gone away, who never tired of doing it, laughing afresh each time at the trick.

When I first came hunting him, hoping he would join me on my new show, he had not got the point. Reluctantly, weeding by Ybarra's grave, he had asked, "What would they think of me?"

"We can find out," I told him. "Think what a grand joke it will be to put Otto Ramirez on the air as a German-tongued farmer. These are the charades you can play with radio."

He had stood up, dusting off his hands on his dark formal pants. "They may not like it if they know who I am."

"Let them hear you and decide."

"It is something I can try."

In the year since, studying his part seriously, he had added the leather breeches and embroidered suspenders, and now considered the role to be his own invention.

"Would she take time to do it?" Returning us to the prospect of this dowager of national acclaim, I was not sure she would be as easy to recruit as Otto had been.

He laughed, sure of his plan. "She would be a surprise to the grandfathers."

"No doubt about that."

Clearing his throat, he produced his last trick. "I told her you would call her."

"You've already arranged it all. That's why you asked me along, to spring the news on me." I laughed at his planning.

"It seemed a good idea." He attempted modesty.

Memorial was flatter, and even more anonymous, than I had imagined. There was no way to read the names of the departed without getting out of your car. If you did not already know where to look, you could walk across fifty identical brass rectangles and never find your kin. I envisioned in the caretaker's office a giant grid similar to a bingo card, with numbers down the rows and letters across the top. Leafing through his files he would tell you, "Your papa is at G-65. If you would care to consult the chart."

Otto, parking his Chevy beside Memorial's meager garden, went off to do his duty. Here among the roses and clipped hedges the bereaved could wander with the funeral director, talking of arrangements, of watertight containers, of where on the bingo chart Mama should go. Left to myself, I inspected a larger-than-life flesh-tinted icon of the Savior smiling from the pages of a behemoth brass-plated Bible. Jesus loves.

Stepping over a low hedge, I mingled with the mourners. Men whose names were Noble and Clarence reassured one another that the deceased had been as good a man as they. "He never went looking for no trouble but he never backed away from it neither." Women called Lurleen and Lavinia decided, dry-eyed, that there was an abundance of food back at the house and they ought to work out a schedule for serving it. "We may as well do it right. After all, that's what we're here for."

The bereaved were all dressed alike. That is, the men were all in one costume; the women in another. As I watched, the men tied on white bricklayers' aprons and black armbands and gathered in a silent semicircle, hands clasped behind them, waiting. Priests before a ritual mass.

Just behind them, the wives, daughters, mothers, aunts stood wrapped in flaring, ankle-length tan wool coats, each with a narrow strip of indeterminate brown fur tacked to its collar. These coats, not needed in the warm early spring weather, seemed left from some past time of prosperity common to them all, a prosperity now diminished, discounted, forgotten, remaining only in these little-used coats too good to discard. Bunched together, the women murmured among themselves, a Greek chorus.

At some signal below the level of my hearing, the two groups stepped forward to the coffin. The man selected by his peers to give the lodge's ritualized and stately words laboriously delivered his memorized oration. That completed, the women, as if on cue, fluttered from their purses tan chiffon squares to tie down their hair, and, at the same instant, the brother Masons fell forward in unison to cast sprigs of evergreen from their pockets onto the coffin. The flurry of scarves and cedar, the choreography of hands lifting and flinging transfixed me.

I strained to capture the now motionless image of aprons and coats, to impress upon my vision this litany of duplication. Then, behind the concordant crowd, a frightened woman with cut-glass eyes moved her narrow head. She was dressed in an elegant gray pin-striped jacket, gray tailored trousers, and a costly yellow silk shirt, garments out of place in this backwater of grief; and looked as if she wished herself many miles from Memorial.

I went up to her as the tan shoulders and banded arms surged forward to embrace the next of kin.

"I'm Avery Krause. From Prince Solms."

"I'm Minna Raabe." She indicated a dumpy woman in the regulation coat. "Do you know my mother? She lives there."

Mother did not wait for introductions. "She never tells me she has friends here," she complained. "She never asks me what she should wear. Not a man's suit you would think to heaven at her own uncle's funeral." Embarrassed, taking advantage of the unexpected appearance of a stranger, she fled to her own kind.

"Mother said don't dress," Minna told me. "'We don't wear black any more,' she said." Miserably, she gestured toward her own visibility. "Out of touch as I am, I believed her."

I tried to shrug it off. "I don't look any better in my jeans."

"At least you look local."

"You don't live here?"

"Washington. I'm down here eating Parker House rolls at Mom's house."

"What are you doing back?"

"Casting an apparent pall." She shuddered. "I think I'll wipe off my lipstick and try to pass as the driver of the hearse. What are my chances?"

"We can go sit by Jesus and the rose bushes."

"If we go off together they'll think we're in drag and up to no good."

"No one will notice. Clarence and Noble and Lavinia and Lurleen are consoling your mother."

Minna found a stone to sit on to protect her pleated pants from the grass. Creasing them anxiously she stared at the crowd. Her face was gaunt and heavily made up. With her hair pulled back into a dark knot, she looked like nothing as much as a skinned rabbit.

"Do you know Mom's brother that we're crating?"

"No. I came with the sexton."

"I don't know him either. I came with the next of kin."

"What did he die from?"

"They never say around here, do they? I suspect it was from caution. My father always warns me, 'Watch out for cars.' Since I was a little girl he says that. When he puts me on the plane for Washington, he warns me, 'Watch out for cars in the big city.' When I drive Mom out here today—he can't come with us naturally because it isn't his family—he tells me, 'Be careful on the highway. Watch out for other drivers.'" She paused. "Around here, I think you die of watching out."

As we talked I put together her familiar name and her East Coast air. It came to me where I had heard of her. "You're the newswoman, aren't you?"

"I'm their token female in medium hard news. At least I was when last in touch with them. You never know from one day to the next where you stand. They think me down here writing an article. They don't know I'm running as fast as I can."

"Willy Vlasig told me about you. I do a radio interview show, in a cow pasture outside of town."

"Quit while you're ahead. Stay in that field. How do you know Willy, our illustrious congressman?"

"I helped with his election."

"Just so he believes he owes it all to you. Tell me about it."

For a change, it was my turn to be interviewed. "I got his opponent on the air, and then, when we were all through with the standard talk and he was about to go, I confided that I had heard a rumor that Willy was going to spring a story at the last minute that his opponent was an alcoholic. I offered to tape a rebuttal, which we could have handy, just in case an accusation broke out the day before the election.

"He fell like a ton of bricks, let me set up the whole thing on a tape which had him denying the false charge that he had ever had a drinking problem. I let Willy send it to all the stations in the district, and, the day before the election, here it came, out of the blue, the man protesting a charge that had never been made. It sank him like a stone. So, naturally, Willy came around to say thanks. I didn't really do it for him; just to see how it would work. I was trying out my wings, to see what radio could do. Anyway, we got to be friends."

"Do you sleep with him?" She studied her long, glazed fingernails.

"No. Do you?"

"Not me. I'm in enough trouble as it is. Although I understand the line reaches around the Capitol."

"His wife must; look at those six blond sons. A regular *Kinderchor*."

"I think he rents those for home visits." Minna loosened up a bit. Shed her jacket and leaned her yellow elbows against it. "Did you know he has a sheep in his office?"

"Willy? I'm not surprised. He drove his office here crazy with sheep tales."

"A real sheep. Stuffed. It's weird. I meet him, Willy, at a party and he finds out we are from the same home town. Small world, he says, so he has me come by his office and meet his staff. We're at your disposal, he says. And there it stands, big as life. A great conversation stopper, he says. Proof that he comes from the hill country."

"He told them all sheep stories at the last of the campaign. His staff had spent months getting him to read up on grazing so he could talk to the ranchers in the part of the district that gets into West Texas. In revenge, at the last, that's all he would talk about. '*Crowpick*,' he'd say, 'is a condition which usually affects the eye sockets.' One of his aides would plead, 'Look, Willy, there are ten little old ladies out here who want to shake your Aryan hand,' and he'd recite, '*Intussusception*, which is also called *gut-tie*, has no particular symptoms except rapid death.'"

Minna creased her trousers again into a thin line as she stared at the Masonic aprons and tan coats. "How do you stand it down here?"

"I came home with Mama when Papa died."

"From where?"

"The mountains of Kentucky."

"That's the frying pan to the fire." She reached into her giant leather saddlebag, pulled out dark glasses to shade her glittering eyes. "My shrink says you come back for the inevitable slap in the face you are due for leaving. Guilt, he tells me, is defiance awaiting retribution." She peered at me through the dark glass. "What's the matter? No one to go back to?"

"There was someone, an actor. Henry. Charles Henry David. Three given names. But I was ready to move on. You can't room indefinitely with a magician."

"Right. Danger always of turning into a rabbit." She looked at the grass. "That's why I'm here eating Parker House rolls. Because I left one up there. A magician, as you might say. At least I hope I've left this time. From a distance it's hard to keep your distance." She fished in her bag for a cigarette. "Did you ever read Sylvia Plath's letters to her mom?"

"No."

"I read them one day at work and began to laugh so hard I had to leave the office. They are my letters home exactly, to a T. Same scene. When I throw myself off the Washington monument, Mom will tell all the neighbors, 'Why, Minna never had an unhappy day in her life.' I'll give you a sample of one of mine." She spread out her bag in front of her as if holding a book and began to read in a chatty, media voice:

" '—Dear Mom,
I got a yellow blouse on sale today at Garfinkel's and white skirt, not on sale. I think with my gray jacket and pants that should take me through the spring. Last night a bunch of us went to see a new musical called FLEECE—'

"I make up the name of the musical as I can't remember what I've told her I'd seen before, and I know she won't know the difference anyway. I named it after Willy's sheep, as you can see. Actually, that is the night I spent helping a friend of mine who calls up to say that she is hanging dolls. She had quit her job and started making rag dolls to sell and that afternoon she has started hanging them by the neck like ball fringe around the ceiling of her apartment.

"'Tonight, Mom, I have a date for dinner in Georgetown, which should be a lot of fun. Got to go now and wash my hair for the big evening.

Love,
Minna Louise—'

"The date means I am picking up some Chinese food on the way home, in case he gets there, or in case we don't get drunk as soon as he does. Typical letter home. I write what Mom wants to hear. When I don't write, she retaliates by losing her voice. Long distance. There I am, company or something—he's finally showed, Saul—and the phone rings and there's this silence, this thick breathing that only a mother can make."

Minna shifted on the grass, careful not to incur grass stain. "It's her way of getting back at Dad. Dad plays chamber music. He lives for his chamber music. So he has to live with someone who doesn't make a sound."

But I turned the talk from mamas back to men. That was safer territory; we all had ticks and cabins in our lives. "Tell me about the man you left."

"I'm carrying on with this man, high up in government, for most of the waking years of my life. That is, to me I'm carrying on all the time. To him it's not that much. His name is Saul. He's married, as they always are; I want him to marry me, as we always do. I order, if you can believe this, from a New York store, stationery with my first name and his last name on it for scratch paper. At Christmas I give myself gift-wrapped boxes of monogrammed towels, with his initials."

I shook my head; I couldn't believe it. This was not something I understood at all. The chief attraction of the mayor, that father of sons, in my life was that he was only in it once a week. The idea of waking up branded Avery Sterling Price made me terrified. The idea of knowing how many pair of white socks he had and whether he kept them rolled or folded or thrown like so many loose noodles in a drawer was unthinkable. Maybe, for Minna, her man was like the hairy belly. Still, who wanted to be married to someone who appeared in top hat one day and as weight lifter the next? I had enough trouble making sense of things without being mated to a quick-change artist.

"I'm in love not only with him but with everything he owns. When he isn't looking, I stroke the fenders of his car. Out of touch as I am, I even love his wife. I save her clippings. Every month she gets her picture in the *Star* attending a style show or a rad chic luncheon for the quality people who aren't eating grapes or lettuce or something." She half closed her eyes and squinted at the mourners. "Do you think she'd mind? That I have a whole scrapbook? Just of her?"

"Do you sleep with him?"

"What do you mean? I do everything with him that's been invented and a lot that's banned. When I get the chance." I couldn't see where she was looking now behind her huge shades or if she were looking at anything at all.

"Sleep, I meant. All night."

"Oh. No. He can never be gone overnight." She lowered her face to her knees and her voice to a whisper. "I hate that closing door when he leaves."

"Or when you have to drive yourself home." Thinking of a few shaggy goats, sandwich crumbs in the car.

"I've never been to his place. He always comes to mine. Until lately, that is. Now he doesn't. He calls with some excuse. He sends flowers. But he doesn't show. The last time he promises to come and I call in sick to be there. I wait all day. No calls but Mom with her gasping voice. I move to a new place with a bed he hasn't used and get an unlisted number. I mail the stationery to his office. Finally, I come home to Mom and her rolls. Take a leave of absence from the paper at least long enough to glue myself back together."

While she creased herself, composed herself, I shared with her the weekend in the hotel room with Sterling. Such a familiar tale she would not have to give it her full attention. His rushing out to meetings and then scurrying back between sessions and after meals, bolting the door, stripping to his socks, pouring a drink, making promises, having at it, retying his tie, wet-combing his hair, making promises, and hurrying out again.

The second day, I told her, I ate a late breakfast alone in the orange-slice decor of the sunny coffee shop. Looking about for my counterparts who must fill the hotel: women of thirty with blond hair and a sudden voracious hunger, sitting singly at tables about the outer edges of the room.

Minna nodded. She had been there, to a hotel like that, with a man just like that. She cut her eyes to Raabe the elder, now seated with identical friends in the funeral home's chairs, talking idly, while dirt and flowers, under Otto's direction, were discreetly piled over the departed.

"I came home," Minna resumed, again in her cool professional voice, "because I began to eat again. The last time I tried to leave him, Saul, I gained sixty pounds. In eight months. An old pattern, the shrink tells me. But what does he know? I was the fat child; he wasn't. It's weird. The thinner I get, the fatter I remember myself. Mom dressed me in gray tents she ran up on her Singer sewing machine. Notice I still know my place and wear the color. She is fond of saying to me that God made the little bird red and the elephant gray. The kids at school used to point at me and holler, 'Here comes Grady, here comes Grady Raabe.' I suppose that's why I thought I was safe in my damned suit today. It should have fit right in." She stared at the tan women. "Back then I wanted a plaid dress more than anything in the world."

"In the mountains we all wore those. We all looked alike."

"You don't know, if you haven't been there, how awful it feels not to be one of the herd. In Washington I look more like everyone else than everyone else, and I keep it that way. Protective coloration."

It was impossible to imagine the elegant, thin woman in front of me fat. I wanted to know her better. Anyone who could shed that gray-tented past, could escape this fatherland and its force-feeding mamas, had to be a winner, and I had a dearth of winners in my life. I wanted to follow my new friend around and method-act what it took to get from a frizzy towhead Swede to such an epitome of self as she presented. Reluctantly, I watched her mom bear down upon us.

Minna got to her feet. "Watch that walk of hers; every step says, 'After all those gray dresses I made for you.'"

"I have some gin, and space, if you get your fill of Parker House rolls at home."

"Thanks for rescuing me today."

"Watch out for cars—"

Her mom stood between us. "She never tells me she has friends." She moved her daughter along. "Down on the grass when there are chairs in plain sight."

Otto was also through. "Now you have seen," he said, when we were back on the road between Veramendi and Prince Solms, "a place with no fences."

"It's not natural." Smiling, I repeated Mama's words.

"Now you see," he agreed.

FIVE

We Do Research

It was St. Patrick's Day before I heard again from the writer. Maybe this was a pattern and I could look forward to Easter, and then the Fourth of July. . . .

I was interviewing the man who dyed San Antonio's river green. The Ear loved the sound of the particular: in this case, the sanitation engineer who actually opened the packet of colored powder. His words had an immediacy and authenticity that we could not achieve interviewing the festive spectacles that delight the Eye: drum majorettes in kelly green sequins, bakers with nine-tiered emerald-iced layer cakes, midget brides and grooms wreathed in clover and dressed in Ireland's own lace and linen.

Asking, in my own way, How is it to create the Venice

of Texas when the shamrock returns? I let the little, fidgeting man tell his story.

This year, he informed us, it took sixteen pounds of dye to do the job.

"And how does that compare?"

"It's up from last year. That's due to the water level."

"Is everyone excited to see it flowing green?"

"They don't care much, the tourists. They don't know the difference. We had some photographers come out and make a bunch of fuss about it. But they were sent out, you know. It wasn't their idea. The city put them up to it."

When the phone rang I eased our guest off with a little mellow Jimmy Buffet—expecting it, of course, to be Sterling, hurt at this casual treatment of the pomp and circumstance of the wearing of the green in his city.

"Good morning, KPAC, Keep Peace."

"This is Gruene Albrech."

"Billy Wayne. I had forgotten you." I lied to gather up my defenses.

"I'm driving to Spreewald tomorrow, because that's the home of the Wends who are the grandfather's villagers. I've done what I can in my head and now I need to see how the place looks. I'm not expecting much: they fought the Germans for centuries over there and then were wiped out by them over here."

"Gone with the Wends."

He became silent. Then, "I thought I'd call."

Princes, I forget, dealing with them so seldom, want you to be serious. "Will you be coming through here?"

"Spreewald is the other direction, east of Austin."

How was I supposed to know? And if he was headed in

the other direction, why had he called? Not, surely, just to report that fact. I offered what came to mind. "Why don't you detour this way for pancakes at the Alpen Haus?"

"I've been eating early, at six o'clock when I get up."

In the pause I seized the remaining seconds. "What's on your mind, Billy? My guest is beginning to gnaw his green fingernails."

"I guess to see if you want to go with me. You may not. It's likely to be an all-day trip."

I let out my breath in relief. "I like all-day trips."

"Most of the time I'll be in the church. That's where most of my story takes place."

"Churches come with cemeteries; I'll content myself with that."

He sounded dismayed. "Don't do that. You can bring along a book or something."

"When do you want to leave?"

"Shall I pick you up after your show? Is that all right?"

"That's a fine time."

Otto smiled his approval as I awkwardly made my date with Billy. Before he went on the air to give another rainless forecast, he said, "It's like I told you."

I wore a dress for Gruene. A green dress (pronounce my name *green* he had said) long-sleeved, round-necked, old. I had worn it for four years; had worn it up and down our hills and on the sides of mountains, too. He might invent himself afresh—name, clothes, personality—I, on the other hand, had been around awhile. Avery yesterday was Avery today. The writer could conclude, if he wished to, that Avery would be the same tomorrow.

Riding in a car is very intimate. There are few distractions; there is little distance between driver and passenger. Each movement of crossing legs or smoothing skirt heightens the atmosphere. Even our exhalations lent a fragrance. Which is to say that, on our way to Spreewald, I was very aware of the writer beside me.

East of Austin we turned off the highway into a two-lane farm-to-market stretch of road that led us past blackland farms patchworked with dairy cows and dotted with the spires of white frame churches.

Admitting to anticipation, I had eaten a doughnut for breakfast instead of my Grape-Nuts; and, almost out the door on the way to the studio had washed my tangled frenzy of hair. Which, to Otto's amusement, I had brushed dry in lazy time to such country smoothies as "Slide off Your Satin Sheets."

Now I was further on edge because of my feeling that with men you either moved closer to them with each meeting or you moved farther apart. This was not based on my experience: the school principal and I ate our apples to the end across the same lunch table; the actor and I did our audacious subterfuges on the same unchanging stage; the mayor and I grew not a goat hair closer for our weekend at the hotel. But, no matter, the feeling feeds on that unreasonable expectation with which we meet each new encounter. I had to believe that more was happening here than a drive to see the grandfather's village.

Crossing onto an even narrower road past a rickety bridge, we left the farmland behind and descended into a sparsely settled, rocky countryside, cut by a small clay-banked creek. Turning to me, Gruene began the story of his Wends. "In the old world they were Serbs. They lived on the Spree River which split into two hundred canals. All their traffic was on flat boats. In summer they raised sky-blue flax. In winter when the ground was crusted they carved wood and wrote their poems. In spring they caught eels and smoked them."

"You've done your research."

"That's all from secondary sources, though. It's time I got a look for myself, at what's left of them. When they lived in Europe the Germans tried to force conversion on them as a means of conquest. For centuries they resisted, shedding blood in order to keep their three- and four-headed gods. But then, I lose track of them. By the time we pick them up here they are fanatical Lutherans, claiming descent from Japheth, the son of Noah. Somehow I have to bridge that gap."

"That's irony."

"I guess the fact that once they fought the Christians and then became them is. But I suspect that nothing very much changed underneath; that only the outward form altered to accommodate their new church rituals."

"You don't have the trouble I do with two things appearing true at once. Obviously not, as you go around being both Gruene and Billy Wayne."

"—You were someone on the phone and someone else on the air."

"Sometimes you play a part. That's different."

"The question is, which is authentic?" He paused. "That's what I'm here to find out."

"Your people are the same as the rest of us; we all have just one primary source."

Gruene let his arm rest on the back of my seat. Not quite touching me, he said, "No one understands that. They go to great lengths to create themselves from other people's notes."

At the outskirts of a shrunken, back-road town, cut off from its neighbors by distance and a brake of trees, he headed the car slowly toward a church towering at the town's center.

Pulling into a deserted churchyard between a field of white headstones to the left and a narrow vaulted church to the right, whose whitewashed plaster echoed both the frescoes of the Middle Ages and the adobe of the Southwest, Gruene let the motor die. He asked, "Do you want to go in with me?"

"You go ahead. I'll come later." I did not want to intrude on the initial vision of his setting; did not want, by the nearness of my pale green-on-green self, to remind him again that two things could take place at once.

In the graveyard, Gruene's Wends lay as they had fallen, each placed beside the next in turn by date of death. It was the first cemetery in my experience where there was no congregation by consanguinity, no sorting of our kin apart from your kin, no segregation by ivy or shells. This was a new idea to me; it raised new possibilities. If last names had no importance, as all belonged to the family of God, then there would be no division into Krauses or Dolles. No need to continue in the afterlife the feuds of this one. All problems such as Mama's would be solved if Uncle lay next to the neighbor who went before him and not beside his ill-wived nephew.

What kinship pattern did exist was in the matter of naming. Each intricately carved headstone repeated over and over essentially the same six given names: Johann, Maria, Christian, Anna, Magdelena, Andreas. Such repetition could only represent place in the family, designating Eldest Son, Eldest Daughter, Second Son, Second Daughter—with those few scattered odd names being the unexpected Fourth or Fifth. I judged Magdelena to be Second Daughter, as Grandmother had been. . . .

In the lower corner the field of headstones trailed off into a patch of blackberries, buttercups, and wild red clover. Sinking to my knees in the wildflowers, I fashioned primrose and clover chains for all the Magdelenas; my fingers, in reflex from years in Kentucky meadows, tying the stem of one blossom about the neck of the next, each round bloom swinging down to wait its turn. With the Second Daughters wreathed, I hung the last about the neck of Avery, Only Daughter, whose dress, stemlike, branch-like, leafed to meet the deep and timid pinks.

Gruene, a pilgrim, stood in the center of his church. Curved walls two feet thick rose from a flagstone floor to high arched windows cased in Dresden blue. A blood-red cantilevered altar held a gold cross-pierced crown. The old colors of flax and berries gave the nave a pagan flavor.

The writer, turning to find me beside him, shook himself back into the rim of the present. "My scene starts here, at a wedding. The grandfather's youngest granddaughter is marrying a German. There is much grief over this. But when it starts we are here; it is too late to stop it. That gives me a chance to show the mix of their Christian and pagan ways. The bride is in black with a crown of myrtle thorns."

"Do we have myrtle in Texas?"

"Something. Agarita. I'll have to see."

He pointed to the high altar. "At the end of the book we are again in the church. It is here, then, that the grandfather, who is their preacher, goes blind."

"Surely they wouldn't harm him in here?"

"He goes blind because he can't bear what he sees before him."

In the front of the church Gruene put a quarter in a tourist information machine which told, in scratchy faint recorded voice, an apocrayphal history of his Wends. In German. "Even their language," he complained. "They stole even the language."

Out in the sun, Gruene looked about, finally noticed my flowers. "Did you make the daisy chain?"

"Yes, I made fourteen of them."

"I haven't seen one in a long time." He looked at me a moment, as if about to say more. Then, apparently deciding he could not admit to even that much past, let it go.

"It was a lovely cemetery. No feuds."

"I don't see the attraction—" He frowned and fell into silence. Then, "I brought us a picnic."

"Can I help with it."

"It isn't much."

He didn't overstate his case. From the car he produced a new straw hamper containing two peanut butter and jelly sandwiches wrapped in paper napkins and a Mason jar of tap water.

"You're right." I smiled at him, imagining Billy Wayne in his standard cowboy clothes in the ordinary act of spreading jelly with a flat kitchen knife. What a small, welcome hole in the dike of his existence.

"Do you mind if we eat over there? I think their good and evil spirits came with them. I want to get the feel of their woods to see."

On a rise behind the church we spread our lunch within a grove of poplar and oak. Around us each tree grew separate from its neighbor; no old country thicketed brake this. I tried to envision his early eel-catchers, immigrants to this flatland, beseeching, from these stunted trees, the gods who once rustled the leaves of their ancestors. It was clear that if they had fled their crusted winter ground for the oppressive heat of Texas they had assimilated at least one thing from the Germans: it did not do to take things easy.

Unable to enter the thread of his story, I played out my own fairy tale—scattering Hansel and Gretel crumbs for the sparrows—and, eating my gummy sandwich, left him alone to make contact with whatever sprites from beside the Spree were stranded in this stand of trees.

Finally, when it looked as if he was lost for the afternoon, I brought us back to the earlier discussion, of whether two things can take place at once. "How can they believe in the gods with all the heads and the Christian God, too?"

"A *god* is simply that which is invoked," he said, looking back at the church. "They must have had the same thing in their minds, here and there, whatever name they gave to it."

"Then we all make gods." In the sense I meant of summoning the other. In the sense that all those words we use for what we want so badly—communion, connection, congress, communication—mean reaching out to what is not-you.

Gruene brushed the dark hair out of his eyes and looked at that thought. "I guess I needed to get the feel of theirs." He washed his lunch down with the lukewarm bottled water. By way of keeping the talk open, he admitted, "Yesterday I tried firsthand some of their rituals. I dyed twelve eggs, the way they did at Easter, with a paste made from red onion skins and hot beeswax. It's supposed to be the color of Christ's blood."

"Gory."

"The Wends were. They healed their sick by piercing the flesh with spring-driven needles and then bathing the wounds with rags soaked in horses' blood."

I had a sudden flash of insight, a clear glimpse of the writer alone on his borrowed acres, enacting those old pagan customs. Using more than his jelly knife. "Where did you stick the spring-driven needle?"

At the question his face closed to mine. "The mattress," he said flatly.

"Now you're being opaque."

"You made fun."

"Somewhat." I shrugged.

It was not true that every time you got together it went somewhere. This was going nowhere. What if he followed me into my garage apartment and watched me remove my old dress, only to decide that I'd grown cloudy and he'd rather not? I was in enough trouble now without taking on a weather report between the sheets.

Tired of this, I threw my jellied crusts down for the birds. Defeated people who let their blood for the old days was an overused plot; we teethed on such stories in Prince Solms. "You villagers are two-time losers," I told him. "The Germans got them going and coming. Why don't you tell us something we don't already know. Why don't you write about winners?"

He packed his picnic basket with the two paper napkins and the water bottle. "You have to write about what is still unsolved for you."

"Tales about losers don't solve anything."

He set down the basket and put his hands on my green-sleeved arms. "Dabney Stuart the poet says, 'There isn't much to be said for winning; you just stand there holding your prizes.'"

"I'm tired of your secondary sources. What does Gruene Albrech say?"

He made a wide-faced smile. "I wondered if you were a prize."

I let out my breath. "You may hold me and see."

So he held me for a while with his solid body which was sturdy enough that it did not matter by which name you called it. Then he kissed me for a while, gently on my mouth. I put my arms around his neck and rested tow hair on his starched blue denim shirt. My waist was higher than his but my shoulders were lower. A nice fit. His breathing was so slow I could hardly feel it.

In my ear he said, "If I hadn't got to do this, I'd have rented my garments."

"Rend?"

"Thriftier to rent."

I looked at his delighted open face. "You practiced that line all morning."

"All month," he admitted.

And then the rest was not of consequence—the sticky sandwiches, the haunted woods. They were not what we had come for; holding fast, we were invoking stirrings of our own.

Back at the car, we leaned awhile against the new fender of his Ford and tried the kissing once again. The arms fell easily into place, and, this time, the legs did, too. There was a certain hang to it which we were getting.

He mashed the buttercups against the branching stem of my dress. "Your neck is pollinated." Tending to that, he touched the hollow of my throat. Then, brushing away the dusty spores of the crushed primrose pinks, he smoothed the green-on-green of my round-necked dress, and me beneath it.

"Nice picnic," I said.

"I wasn't sure you wanted to come."

"I wasn't sure you wanted me to."

"I did."

We rode in silence until the land began to climb again and the fields to grow more fertile. After the reaching spires and the wading knobby-kneed dairy cows, he glanced at me. "Avery?"

"I'm not like you; I only have one name."

"What about the mayor?"

"He is just renting space."

"Rend?"

"Actually, it's more of a loan."

"Alone?"

"Very much. And you?"

"When my woman lived with me I kept getting mixed

77

up about if I was in the room or in the book. When I tried to write, she was in the room, even when she wasn't. When she was not talking, I could still hear her. I got to the point where all the words had been used before, and when I was getting set to use them again, she would whisper, 'Can I bring you something, Billy?' She breathed my air. It was toxic and unproductive. I began to shout at her. So now I try to stay most of the time in the book and forget there is a room around it."

"Do you sleep alone?"

"I've got a dog." He did not misunderstand me.

"What does he do while you write?"

"Works. He works. He smells around and barks at the cows."

"My grandfather has a setter that scratches."

"He only scratches to get in or out. I don't let him have fleas."

"He is not in your room?"

"Even when he is."

"I don't live in my apartment; I live on the radio."

"It's something like that; I don't live in the room, but in the book."

"—I don't have a dog."

"You don't sleep alone." He kept his eyes on the road.

"Oh, but I do."

"All the time?"

"All the time."

He turned us onto the road that led back home, away from the river-bottom farmlands toward our hills. "What about tonight?"

"Do I have to do the asking?"

"If it's your space."

I studied my knees. "All right, Billy. I invoke you to inhabit it."

He ran his hand down the edge of my clean hair. "I don't mean to make you stick your neck out. I'm not very good at this. I'm trying to say I want to spend the night with you. I'm also trying to say if you don't want me to I can go away."

Up the stairs, under the lagustrum, in my blue-walled apartment, he said, "I couldn't tell what you were thinking."

"When?"

"In the car."

"I thought I was transparent enough."

"No. You turn your face away and hide yourself."

"Am I now?"

"You come and go." Gruene stared about the small apartment. "Can we make a drink?"

"I have gin."

He fixed us each one, on ice. Straight.

"I never had it this way."

"Time you did. The taste is juniper." He drained his and fixed himself another, this time double. Strange behavior for a man who picnics on tap water.

But there had been a shift between us. For one thing, he was not talking. He went into the bathroom and peed, not closing the door. Reappearing, he asked, "Where do you keep the bed?"

"Behind the screen."

"We might as well try it." He led me to the double bed and pulled back its bright blue spread.

Awkwardly we sat facing one another, neither of us being good at this. It was too easy to make a wrong move when you were being who you were.

I propped the pillows for us to lean against, and picked a place to begin. "It took me a long time," I told him, "to figure out that I was not the rest of them. When I was ten we moved from Prince Solms to a mining camp in eastern Kentucky where my papa kept books. Every other kid looked just like me: the light hair, the blue eyes, the skinny arms. My parents were the same as theirs: when my mama hugged me it felt like a feather bed; my papa's face looked all the time as if he wished he weren't there.

"We all wore cheap plaid dresses from the general store. At recess it was hard to tell myself from the others. In the afternoons, to be different, I hung my dress on a tree limb and played in the meadow in my underpants." I unbuttoned my green dress to show Gruene where once a dingy sun had tanned me.

"Did they whip you for it?"

"Mama? Papa? No." What a bad thing to be his first thought.

"Go on."

"I'm still trying to figure what is me."

"I was whipped with a belt." He took off his shirt so that I could imagine stripes. "On the back."

"I didn't ask."

"I'm telling. Don't you want to hear?"

"I hear."

"With the buckle." Painfully he spit out this piece of an earlier time.

"By your father?"

"Skip my parents, all right?" He took off my dress, and then my underpants, and pulled me close enough to stroke me. "You have a bathing-suit line. Does that still make you the same as every other blonde around?"

"All of them don't live at Pasture Radio."

"Then I know how to tell which is you." He kissed me slowly. "When I used to sleep with my brother, we tied a string down the middle of the bed to make sure we each stayed on our own side."

"Did you bring twine with you?"

"If I'd wanted to sleep with a string down the middle of the bed I would still be sleeping with my brother."

"I'm glad you're not."

"So is he." He took off his trousers and new undershorts. Pulling me close until my face was buried against his neck, he said, "My dog sleeps at the foot of the bed."

"Not me."

"He keeps my feet warm."

"Put on your socks."

"He's got this great coat of hair."

"Quit pimping for your hound, Billy Wayne."

Rubbing my hips with both hands, he told the rest of the story about the earlier woman. "She made sex into the big finale. It got to where I couldn't write after supper, knowing she was waiting, then I couldn't write in the afternoon. Once lunch was over she would start to get her black things out and plump the pillows. Then I couldn't work at all. Every night when the big moment came I shut my eyes and masturbated between her legs, pretending she was the Italian woman in her satin slip I had wanted at seventeen." Holding me tight, he forced out the words, "I don't want to do that with you."

"I don't want to do the shopkeeper with you," I whispered.

"With the mayor?"

"Yes."

"How often?"

"There is a weekly trek down a dirt road. Past some goats."

"Do you want to try?" His voice muffled in my hair.

"I'm not asking, Gruene."

"I'm asking. Don't you hear? I'm asking."

I pressed my hands against his shoulders, reminding myself they were his, no fantasy. "How does it work this way?"

"I don't know. That's what we're here to find out."

"Are you sure?"

"I have to be, don't I, if I'm here?"

Tentatively, as he opened my lips and then the rest of me, I held tight to the body with bowed legs and once-scarred back. Thick and immediate, he was not Billy and he was not Gruene: he was real.

We found you could do all the same things, in the same way, yet have it not the same at all. (For me, it was the difference between taking off my shirt for the school nurse in her office behind the lunchroom, and taking off my shirt to run bare through a field of goldenrod beside the trailer.)

In the shopkeeper scene you were removing yourself as far as possible from the man handling you; you were acting a movie in which he was not even a player. And he (if he were the mayor) watched his own pornography behind quivering, titillated eyelids. Each of you escaped the other, leaving only your bodies behind engaged in the most manual of labors.

When you were with someone who was in you and with you and around you and he was also who you wanted to be with and around and in, as here, you realized that the blurring of what was you and not-you, the transcending of your separate limits, was what made love.

Late in the night, asleep, he rolled back across an old string, where, motionless, with ankles locked together and arms crossed on his chest, he returned to the past and covered himself.

SIX

In the Coal-burning State

Lying in bed working out the boundaries of my self before going to Mama's for the Sunday meal, I found I missed, severely, incredibly, the body of the writer.

Not Billy Wayne the Czech with his rodeo rider's golden body or Gruene the expatriate wrestling with the grandfather grown ill at the sight of his flock, but that belt-whipped, juniper-drinking, solid nameless man.

I had not heard from him in ten days. A time span which included a raft of morning interviews, and one more shabby trip to the mayor's cabin on the wrong side of the Medina River.

The night with the writer had brought back to me a time, specifically one dance, with the first boy I ever cared about, in high school in Kentucky.

I sat in class behind a dark boy with short legs and a thick barrel chest. Seated alphabetically—his name was Ralph Kingsley Kenedy—we spent most of the day a desk apart. He did not care for school; did not do well at it. Did not hear the covert clues the teachers gave for getting out and away as opposed to giving in and up. Headed for the mine shafts where his father and his grandfather worked, he saw his classes as a drawn-out delay of the inevitable.

He was never absent—as truancy garnered the obvious reaction that if you're not in school, boy, you may as well be at work—yet he was never really present either. I used to wonder where he was, inside his head. It was hard for me to imagine the private self of people who had few words; I thought it possible they dealt with the alteration of spaces rather than the reeling of scenes. I supposed them to think with their bodies.

He looked at me a lot, as if considering how we had happened to intersect; not as if he had in mind or knew how to do anything about it. While I did my lessons—pages of paper work assigned to do in school as the teachers did not believe we could complete work once we were sucked back into our own environment out of theirs—he turned and watched me. Not passing judgment on my industry or his lack of it; just watching.

I was too shy to look back at him, but I thought a lot about how it would feel to touch him, to get the sense of him that way. I wanted to be his girl, as that was defined in the mountains; which was mostly standing around after school until time to feel around after dark.

But by that time my light eyes and frizzled hair were no longer enough disguise to let me pass for any mountain girl. My sharp features too often bent over books had put a distance. I did not date; had not even been kissed.

Those were the years that Mama and Papa bartered over a house in town. When we first moved to Kentucky we lived in a trailer in a row of no-longer mobile homes stretched a meadow away from a tributary of the Poor Fork River. As the other families did, we grew tiny tended patches of beans tethered on strings, radishes, and lettuces, corn if there was space. By the front stoop, rows of marigolds turned sun color in the heat beside shoots of tough-stemmed zinnias. In the field behind the trailers, goldenrod and Queen Anne's lace grew wild as other people's children.

Mama had hated the trailer with its crumbling privy in the back and its old path through the field for carrying water from the creek. She thought herself entitled to a real house in town, with a proper garden in which to display a varied bouquet of bachelor buttons, pinks, climbing sweet peas, stock, larkspur, nasturtiums, snapdragons, sweet alyssum. She wanted a window box for white and purple pansies, and space for a new cook stove near whose warmth the dough could rise, and a back porch with room to set cakes to cool or milk to clabber.

Papa had not wanted to tie himself further to that alien place whose soot and grime stained even his collars as he bent over his books. For five years they argued: whenever Mama began a baby, Papa promised the larger space if, this time, there was need of it. Then, each time she lay back, emptied, on her cramped trailer bed, her house was forfeited.

Finally, Papa came to view it the other way around. It

might be, he considered, that Mama did not have the son because she did not have the house. For a year he negotiated for a brick-faced place in the dingy company town; money had to be pried loose long distance from the Germans, loans obtained from canny mountain bankers.

The year I finished eighth grade, Mama got her flower box, set below a kitchen window which framed the black drift-mouth of the mine. There, in her new house, she made sweets and songs. She served us late afternoon lemonade with intricate crisp and lacy cookies from the oven. She iced airy angel cakes whose candied violets pushed (like alpine flowers) through the snowy boiled frosting. On Sundays, she settled on the porch swing in the dusty filtered light and dropped into Mason jars of water those fragile paper flowers that open when wet into lily pads. Transfixed by this repeated miracle, she would push herself back and forth with her tiny white-shod feet, and hum her little hymnal tunes.

Papa shut his ears to her Swedish songs; refused to eat her decorated confections. He could not grow accustomed to a house in which the wife pleased herself—it was not the German way.

(I do not know, as I could no longer hear the muffled sounds of covers or nightclothes as I had in the trailer, whether Papa tried each night in that new house to shove a son up Mama. To get what he had paid so dearly for.)

The spring of our senior year in high school the teachers promised us a formal dance—some conviction on their part that those days of nylon net and split carnations had been a factor in their raised expectations, and so might be in ours. Obediently, the whole town set out to comply with their dream. Mamas turned tired hands to piece goods by the yard. Papas worked overtime, and did without the evening beer in the back of the general store, to pay the bills.

"There is a dance," Mama fretted. "Who will ask you to go?"

"She has no business to go with anyone in this town." Papa looked up from his books, fearful that I would take us the final step away from his beginnings.

"She can't stay home if there is a dance. It isn't natural. What would people think?"

"That she is too good for this town."

"That she had a mother who would not make her a dress. But I can do that. I have my machine. I can read the patterns. It must be many layers of net."

"Don't put your eyes out over this, Dolly."

"Someone will ask my Avery."

Someone did. I can't remember either his face or his name. Anything about him except that he was the only other student in school headed for college. Maybe his parents, as fearful as mine, had instructed him: never mind that Rose Marie, she is no good for you, she'll only get in trouble. She's a nothing. Ask that nice Avery Krause. She's going to Murray College.

Whoever he was—editor of the paper? captain of the team?—he must have made his family as relieved as mine. I accepted the invitation thinking at least I might see Ralph Kenedy there. I don't know who he went to see.

"Maybe you will have a house like this." Mama had us married at once in her mind, as her fingers began to fly across the yards of blue net.

"Not in this place she won't." Papa's pinched lips turned down as Mama's excitement mounted.

"Who is this boy?" he asked me. We sat on the chintz couch in the living room, crowded with Mama's china-cup collection, pictures of Texas bluebonnets, crocheted arm rests, empty painted vases—all those keepsakes which Mama loved. The muscle in his jaw twitched.

"He's a good student."

"Have you been seeing him on the sly?"

"No, Papa. I'm just going with him to the dance."

"You can't trust a boy that age."

"We'll be in a room with twenty-four chaperones."

"On the way home."

"He doesn't have a car. His papa's taking us."

"Good. The man has sense."

"He's going to Berea College, on a work program."

"But not money, then."

"Papa, I'm just going to a dance."

"Which this town has gone mad over. Just like your mother."

"It was the teachers' idea."

"They should be pushing the books."

"I think he's the valedictorian."

"Well, then."

The morning of the dance, a Friday, Ralph leaned over my desk. His dark face was red. "You goin'?"

"Yes." I didn't make him spell it out. "Are you?"

"Goin' stag."

"I'll see you there . . . ?" My sallow face felt hot.

"Maybe."

My date pinned a tufted, bow-tied clutch of pink carnations on the itchy blue net, which was wide as our hallway and stiff as chicken wire.

Mama splashed unashamed tears down her white powdered cheeks. She leaned over to smell the corsage. "That's a nice thing to do, son," she told my date. Gripping me in her fleshy arms, she said, "You look pretty as a picture."

"Be careful," Papa said. "Don't keep her out late."

"No, sir." The captain, or the editor, whoever he was who held me by the hand as if we both might bolt and run if he did not, propelled me to the car where his dad, equally edgy, waited behind the wheel.

The floodlit gym was packed with as many adults as there were students. Grownups, sipping Hawaiian punch, came to daydream about what they had once had, or, in the case of many of those raised there, had never had. At each dance they pushed us: "Why don't you young folks get out there to that nice music."

We mostly stood around. The couples who were going together tried to figure how to get outside to a car, theirs or someone else's left unlocked. Those come with strangers struggled as we did to make some talk about the public parts of our lives.

"You going to Murray?"

"Yes."

"Where's that?"

"Western part of the state."

"You're lucky then."

"I guess."

"What do you want to do?"

"I'd like to be an actress. But I guess there's no future in that. Not unless you're Sarah Bernhardt or something.

Maybe I'll teach acting or whatever they call it with kids. What do you want to do?"

"My folks want me to be a pharmacist. I don't know. I'm pretty tired of school."

Dutifully we moved around the dance floor, drenching each other with sweat. His palms were wet and he kept wiping them on his suit pants, and then I would wipe mine on my scratchy dress, reducing those damp spots to the limp texture of net curtains.

"What does your dad do?"

"He's an accountant."

"That's how you're going to Murray. Mine's the mail-man."

"Berea is a wonderful college."

"I hear. My parents are kind of proud about it."

It was the last dance, a dreamy two-step from the teachers' past, before Ralph, short and stocky, shoved his way to where I was.

"You want to dance?" He faced me at the edge of the crowd, his back to my date.

"Hello, Ralph."

"This one's mine." My partner roused himself. "Last dance, you know."

"It's all right," I told him, "I promised it to Ralph."

It must have been the first time either of us had made contact in that isolated, predetermining town; we held each other as if it would be the only time.

One hand pressed mine close to his side, his other wrapped around my back until his fingers slid under my arm and held my breasts flat against his chest. Keeping his cheek tight on mine, he led with his thighs, pushing my legs with his. Bending me slightly backward he left no space between us. His erection was there, through the net, as we barely rocked back and forth in the center of the dance floor.

At first I thought I couldn't breathe, but then, giving in to it, I put my other hand tight on his bare neck.

When the music quit, I was the one with no words.

He had rehearsed his. "I may not know how to talk to you, but I know what to do out there."

"Talking isn't that much."

"Maybe." But as he gave me back to my date, it was clear that he had been taught it was.

I went off to college with the feel of Ralph's dark cheek and heavy body against me, wild with not knowing what came after that. Resolved that standing about, expectant as Mama, led only to clabbered milk and window boxes. Resolved, instead, to let myself be entered by the first boy who asked.

The first one turned out to be a tall, lanky fellow who knew what he was about. Moving from brushing my arm in class to loitering by my door at the dorm, he took me out for a Coke, which, as we got acquainted, he laced with a little Bourbon. When that had warmed things, he parked his fancy car beneath a hickory tree and spread us out a blanket. Even before he had kissed the inside of my mouth and unfastened my bra and pulled down my panties, I was ready: trembling not in fear (as he assumed) but in relief that I was finally going to know what it was all about.

"You're the kind of girl I really respect, you know? Let

me take those off, hear? You know you're really beautiful, don't you? I really go for blondes."

It took me a while to understand that his murmurings were whispered not to me but to some movie in his head for which I was the fair-haired surrogate. But by then it was too late; his lanky length had already pushed inside me. By then, lying flat on the weedy ground, I was crying. No one had entered Avery after all.

No wonder Charles Henry David, the actor, when he finally came along, had seemed the prince indeed. With him I did not have to worry about what was real, as anything could be invented or transformed, and was. The play was the thing; and the play was full of his outrageous tricks. "Do I have a volunteer from the audience?" he would ask me as we lay naked together in that mountain bed. Taking my lipstick, he might draw a large, lashed eye around his navel to let me wink at it, or a flat bowed mouth, puckered up for my kiss. A flat red penis, sketched almost to his collar bone, grew long for me. All these images played on his hairy belly as a prelude to grease-smearing laughter, sex, and sleeping.

After five years of such extravagance, it had felt safe and ordinary to get down off the stage with the mayor. What, I had asked myself, could be more real than a burgher in white socks, his wallet gorged with snapshots of Clarence and Alfred?

Now the writer had reminded me that I gave more of myself in that high school gym in Harlan County than I have given in all the years since.

Headed, in his own way, for the mind shafts, Gruene

had reached me. It no longer mattered to me whether he wrote well or not; that was his private confrontation, his personal way to set his boundaries. Locked together we had had no need of his written pages or of my voice over the Mole's airways. We had proved it possible to reach someone, as I had done with Ralph Kingsley Kenedy long ago, without words.

So I had come full circle. To find, in the rumpled bed of my blue-walled garage apartment, that what was me was less than whole, locked in its single boundaries.

SEVEN

Glimpses of Grandmother

"I'm quoting word for word. We're in the grocery trying to decide whether to buy a box of out-of-state strawberries on special for seventy-nine cents. Mom says, 'I don't know . . . it seems to me . . . what do you think . . . I can't decide . . . one has to think . . . last year I waited . . . I don't know . . . How can you know?' Cement. Dealing with her is having your legs set in cement."

Minna was in gray trousers and a brown T-shirt. It, her bag, and her brown leather belt were all designer initialed. With her skinned-back hair twisted into a tight figure eight, it was all very East Coast. All very conspicuous in Prince Solms, but I didn't remind her of that.

We had stopped for potato pancakes at the Alpen Haus

after my show, not wanting to arrive too early at our destination: the house of Queen Esther of the Missionary Baptist Church who lived, in fine biblical overtones, on Flood Street.

"Did you buy the strawberries?"

"How can you expect me to remember? We did or we didn't and it took thirty minutes. The thing that gets me is that Mom came into this world with so much going for her. Her mother had four daughters and named them for the most prominent women on the library shelf: Anna, Emma, Tess, and Kristin. Never mind that they had all been raped, seduced, manipulated, married, and abandoned, they were heroines to her. If books had been named for them, they must be. Then along comes Tess, my mom, and names her only child Minna Louise for her mother-in-law. So I can be sure to inherit all the Raabes's cut glass."

Thus explaining the constant need to shade her glittering eyes.

"While we're on the subject of mothers, my mama's digging up Papa. Taking him away from the Germans."

"If you ask me they had him long enough." Minna shoved away a mound of uneaten cakes and syrup. "You can't be serious. I thought that was against the law. Grave robbing or something."

"Otto arranged it with her."

"It raises wonderful possibilities. This year of the Cat, you can lie beside the goldfish pond; next year, in the Dragon, we'll move you over to the chrysanthemum bed."

"It's a family feud."

"But with such class. I'm taking notes down here on how to get revenge. Will add your mom to my list." She fished out a cigarette. "To change the subject, I got a good one for our Willy. I saw where one of your local politicians was fasting until his bills were brought out of committee before the House. I thought this opened fabulous possibilities for manipulation in the big Congress. You could threaten to amputate a finger, or to cut off an ear. Picture the poor subcommittee chairman—one member is promising if this goes out on the floor I'll poison my dog; the other is threatening if you do I'll give myself beriberi."

"You've been eating too many Parker House rolls."

"I don't notice you missing the cookie monster's Sunday dumplings."

"I don't notice that either—"

Minna looked somewhere over my head. "Do you know what the paper thinks I'm doing down here?"

"Not comparison shopping for strawberries."

"They believe me to be doing an in-depth study of penile implants."

"You're kidding."

"You may not be aware that Baylor Medical School in Houston is a pioneer in creating the artificial erection for organic impotence."

"I was unaware."

"The grandfathers would be wild to know. If you want to be the one to tell them. Surprised the mayor hasn't mentioned it."

"When your article comes out his will be the first phone call reminding me he doesn't have that problem."

"Why do you stick with that guy?"

"Do you want to talk about monogrammed stationery and towels?"

"It's easier to throw stones. Besides, I think I'm through with that. But to continue, there's a device which pumps seventy cc's of radio-opaque solution into a prosthesis. Very discreet. Small button to raise and lower the scaffold. Tucked into the scrotum."

"How do they know it isn't all in his mind?"

"They measure it while he sleeps. I'm going to make a trip down there to watch the noctural penile tumescence, as it were. Maybe I'll work up a slide presentation. I can't stay down here in the boonies indefinitely without something to show."

I accepted one more cup of coffee from the alpine-costumed waitress, knowing it to be one too many. "I still haven't heard from the writer."

Minna lit what was at least her tenth cigarette. Leaning back, she balanced an elbow on the back of the chair. "Writers are so full of themselves they are like dogs looking for fire hydrants. I regularly interview two kinds. There's the best-selling author of *Nasal Catarrh* who has brought along his nine-hundred-and-seventy-eight-page original manuscript so I can touch it reverently. He drops names every time he opens his mouth: he uses Hemingway's typist, he plays tennis with John Updike, right now he's sleeping with one of Scott Fitzgerald's mistresses—"

"This one even dropped his own name."

"Or I get the three-name female. She's Elberta Cling Freestone from Macon, Georgia, who's just done a terribly sensitive but terribly dirty book. She has false eyelashes and hair down to here."

"I'm glad you're going with me to see Queen Esther. I can't envision myself knocking on her door and saying,

'How would you like to be a bit player on Pasture Radio? I'm casting the part now, casting about for someone large, black, and wearing semiprecious stones.' "

"Afraid she'll take a knife to you?"

"I couldn't blame her."

"Actually, it's a trade. I'll hold your hand while the black attacks, if next Wednesday you'll go to San Antonio with me for a media assault. I'm going to be on Terry Lynn Taylor's TV interview show, called, if you can believe it, 'High Noon.' Although I can believe anything in these parts."

"Shall I have the mayor roll out the red carpet for us?"

"Let's skip that." She put out the last cigarette in her pack. "How come you never offered to interview me on your show?"

"You're not right for radio. All your tricks are visual. On radio you have to do some variation on the obscene phone call, some modification of the breathing in the Ear. I comb the papers all the time for ideas. I'll give you two from today's. There's a woman who has set up a corporation to read pornography to the blind. She claims that the sightless are being denied their basic right to squirm and pant with the rest of us. Imagine how salacious her talking sex would be to you, the blind listener.

"Then, there is the doctor who advocates the eradication of all household pets, as the world has become too crowded for nonproducing animals. 'Modern China,' he says, 'took the ultimate step when it eliminated four-legged pets.' Think of how that would appeal to the grandfathers: children could be taught to sniff out dogs in attics and closets. Grandfather's old hound, hidden in Grandmother's washhouse, would be heard in the night, scratching his fleas, and be carried off to the ovens. On radio the horror could mount as if it were a late, late show. But, on television, it would lose its impact when you saw the doctor was just your neighbor, the one who prunes his petunias."

"I'll see what I can bring you back on implants that you could use. Maybe the sound of a sleeper getting a hardon? A sort of beep, beep?"

"What are you supposed to talk about on 'High Noon'?"

"I thought I'd get into good old Willy and his sheep. Let them think I'm his mistress. That'll get him a lot of votes in the district."

"'Good morning, out there in video land, this morning we have as our guest a good friend of our own Willy Vlasig, a personal confidante of the elected official from the town of two rivers.'"

Minna got to her feet. "Let's get out of here. You're getting coffee nerves; and I'm getting lung cancer."

"Queen Esther awaits."

I drove across the broad back of Corn Hill to a frame house on Flood Street, which had the same tin roof, wide-railed porch, and fenced vegetable garden of its neighbors. In the front, a stooped white yardman tended oleander bushes.

"He's deaf," an imposing woman told us from the doorway, "and dumb, too, as most Swedes are."

"I'm Avery Krause. Otto said he had talked to you? This is Minna Raabe, a newswoman from Washington."

"My name is Jane Brown," she informed us. "Queen

Esther is the manner in which the church refers to me." The elderly woman stared at us through gold-rimmed glasses set slightly forward on her nose. As she shook our hands she studied us carefully; we were students in a principal's office.

We were led into a dim and cluttered living room. Her house was not in the German style of company parlor set across a hallway from family room. Rather, we were at once in the presence of her best possessions. Behind the velvet-covered couch was a lace-clothed dining table on which a silver vase held cut pink and orange gladioli. To one side a whatnot shelf displayed a collection of china dogs; on the facing wall framed photographs revealed our hostess in her moments of glory: receiving a commendation from the Cancer Society; presiding over the Court of Calanthe.

Through a beaded-glass curtain behind the dining table I could see a man stretched out motionless on a bed.

Our hostess peered at Minna. "Don't I know you from somewhere? Were you a student of mine? I had an integrated school for one year before they retired me without cause."

Minna shook her head.

"We'll get back to that." Indicating that we should be seated, she turned to me. "Now you're the one with the radio show?"

"Yes, ma'am." She looked exactly as I had hoped; over her black crepe dress she wore a matching cape caught with a brooch of garnets. When she sat, her ample bosom and slightly spread knees made her an imposing figure. Her voice was unexpected: deep, husky, and clearly cultured.

She bent toward me. "I knew your grandmother. She lived right over there behind this house until she married. That's a fact. Our yards adjoined."

A rush of Grandmother's diatribes against black families came back to me: they washed their clothes only on Monday and so the poor men had to wear clothes stale with sweat all week. They never set a proper table, so that the men sometimes had to make do with a supper of cold corn bread and buttermilk.

Jane Brown continued with no notice of my sudden flush. "Your grandmother and I were the same age which ought to tell you something about the Germans. I'm alive and she's been dead these fifteen years. While she was washing the threads from those clothes of hers, I was gaining a statewide reputation for myself in the field of Negro education. I have served on the boards of directors of seven national organizations. What kind of name did your grandmother get for herself out there in that washhouse? The German women have no inclination toward progress. Why, they were scared to death at the idea of an electric wringer washing machine, afraid they'd get their hair caught and scalp themselves. They did their wash in those tubs for years after we had our Sears, Roebuck models."

Dismissing my grandmother and her ilk, she gave us her own history: the necessity to get out of Texas; the achievement of a degree from Howard; the obligation to return here, where she came from. It didn't do to run away. The rise to principal; the firing after integration. The national philanthropies and crusades.

"Your voice would be wonderful on the air." I had cast her already in the part.

"I'm informed it is." Pivoting back to Minna, she pressed. "I have the distinct impression you were in my school."

Minna dropped her cut-glass eyes from wall to patterned rug. Her voice came out a low monotone. "I know where we met, Mrs. Brown. I recognized you when we came in. You are right that it was your school building. It was at Miss Knadle's piano recital in 1950. Not an evening I like to remember."

"Getting fired from the school system which had been my life's work is not something I care to remember, child, but that's where we get our strength. From the reverses." She peered closely at the young woman with the pulled-back hair. "You were the fat girl."

Minna flinched. "You have it. I was the one in the gray satin tent."

"You were the only student in the recital hall who had a grain of talent, inherited from your father and his chamber music, I assumed. I said to myself that night that you would go far in this world. When you played your Bach on that out-of-tune instrument it was a major event in the life of that school." She spoke sharply. "I expected you would be a concert pianist by now."

"I never played again, Mrs. Brown."

"The other girls had no skill and no ear."

"They had nylon net formals. One of them had a pink net dress. I wanted to be the girl in that pink dress more than anything in my life. What difference did it make that she missed every other note in that idiot gavotte?"

"I never would have guessed you to be stupid."

I said, "The girl in pink went home and cried because she couldn't play as well as you."

Minna glanced up. "She was a fool, then."

Jane continued firmly, her tone a reprimand. "In my day we used the talents provided us." She puffed on a cigarette in an ivory holder, sending a wave of smoke over her head. "I think you would both be interested in an experience my boy Theodore had. It provided one of those reversals from which we get our strength. He was in sports; you had to be in sports to get ahead in that day and time. He was in the Junior Olympic program and won the semifinals at the district level in his race which was the one-hundred-yard dash. This qualified him to go to Hattiesburg, Mississippi, to compete for a national slot. He won first place again, but this time there happened to be a German boy who came in second, a classmate of his from Prince Solms. A boy who had the same coach. Now because that child was the only white in the race and the race was held in that particular state, the German boy instead of Theodore was on the front page of their sports section as well as of our paper here. My Theodore thought that a disgrace and he made a loud fuss about it. At first he had his mind set on leaving Sophie County altogether, but I persuaded him that it didn't do to run away. You had to stick it out. So, when the old coach retired and my boy applied for the job, times had changed and they were anxious to show that this was true. That early discrimination against him actually worked to get him his present job as basketball coach at Consolidated High."

Minna got the message. Not meeting Jane's eyes, she said, "Maybe he should have got away. I'm glad I did."

Rising slowly on stiff arthritic legs, Jane indicated the discussion was over. It was time for refreshments. "The silver service is on the sideboard. Shall we go in?"

She served us coffee from hand-tinted heirloom cups and a chocolate cake with the deep, sweet taste of dates. Eating slowly and attentively, serving herself generously to the heavy cream, the sugar cubes, and a second helping of her rich chewy cake, our hostess set the model. I tried to follow her lead as best I could, on top of half an Alpen Haus waffle. Minna did not take a bite.

"Now then, young lady, tell me about your show." The past accounted for, she got down to business.

A room away, through the swaying curtain, the man was reading a newspaper on the bed.

I wiped chocolate from my mouth, which had gone dry. "I thought you and Otto and I would make a perfect team on my show, with me doing the interview, Otto the news and weather, and you the women's events. If you feel you could block out the time." My voice trailed off.

"I'm sure your Otto told you I keep myself busy."

"We could benefit from your national name."

"You mean, child, that the Germans could raise no objection to me."

I smiled. "That, too."

She added a jot of heavy cream to her cup. "It might be a challenge and I have never been one to avoid a challenge. It might be of interest to show what our women are doing. That is a subject of some concern to me. When I was principal I had ample opportunity to see the way the two cultures worked against one another. Our superintendent had a habit of confiding in me, in his guttural tones, that the

Mexicans would never get anywhere until they gave up their Spanish language. Then, in the next breath, he would invite me to share his sorrow that his own children would not preserve their native tongue. All the while both groups of them belittled the other for clinging to the old ways.

"That's why our race is rising to the forefront today; we have the women. A demonstrable fact they fail to consider as they fight battles among themselves for control of their piddling three-hill town. They forget to ask who at the time of the War Between the States ordered a machine from Europe to make newsprint from cornshucks. They don't see what lies beneath their noses. We have the women; one day we will have the power."

Minna pushed away her untouched cake. "I don't believe any of us will ever have power."

"My dear, you don't wish to." Jane Brown finished the last crumbs from her china plate. The repast was over. "Now, then, Avery, I believe I would enjoy the opportunity to play Queen Esther on your show." She let me know she understood the role that had been offered. "But I want it understood that if I do it, I intend to do it all the way."

"That would be wonderful."

"Give me a few weeks to clear the time."

"Whenever you're ready."

Adjusting her brooch, she got ready to dismiss us. "You might be interested in a final anecdote about your grandmother. This one concerns the marriage of her sister Tillie."

I nodded, although I knew that I was not.

"Tillie was my favorite of the two as she was not as

spoiled as Magdelena. She was a goodhearted girl who did what she was asked. When your grandmother got married and moved up to River Hill, she took Tillie along, as it was the custom in those days for an unmarried woman to be part of the work force of the household until she could get a man of her own. As the Krauses at that time had about a dozen men to wait on, Tillie was worked, so they told me, no better than a farmhand. For ten years she made eight loaves a day of salt-rising bread on log coals the same way her mother before her had made adobe bricks for the early church.

"Then, one Sunday afternoon, the way it was related to me, a Lutheran preacher from Veramendi came to town looking for a replacement for his wife who had that month died in childbirth. Your grandfather, that shortsighted man, brought him around to meet their Tillie and that was the end of that. We conjectured here on Corn Hill about which had made your grandmother the angriest: the fact that her only sister left the Reform Church to join the Lutherans, or the fact that she lost her live-in domestic help."

"I hadn't heard that story." There was no keeping the defensiveness out of my voice. I could see Grandmother at the copper washtub, wringing the steaming clothes; could see her in the back yard, wringing the chickens' necks. She used to say that those women who had to get blacks or Swedes to do their work for them were white trash. How could she have treated her own sister that way?

"No doubt. The Germans are a closemouthed lot." But the older woman, stiffly concluding our visit, took note of my distress. In parting she softened her judgment. "Your grandmother and I may have fought in different battles, child, but we never forgot we were in the same war."

I drove around the block behind Jane Brown's house to see where Grandmother Magdelena had lived. The corner house advertised WILL DO IRONING, BABY SITTING, DEER PROCESSED, on a plank nailed beneath two canary cages, above a spread of morning-glories.

In the middle of the block I stopped at what would have been the house: a board and mortar fachwerk house, scalloped with gingerbread, weathered and in need of paint. One one side a chainlink fence enclosed a flock of white hens; on the other a mass of hollyhocks pressed against the window ledge.

Minna put on her dark covering sunglasses. "I can see her in that same cape, at that old school, huge as a house. It must have been a big deal for her to present Miss Knadle's piano recital there, although that didn't dawn on me at the time. All I wanted was to get out of there when it was over. Mom was tagging after me with her talk of the little red bird and the gray elephant and we run smack into this bulwark of a woman who won't let us pass. 'I'm the principal,' she tells Mom, who thinks all principals are white and fatherly and so does not believe her. I thought I would die of embarrassment if I was caught in my big tent of a dress talking to someone with a lard-tub body just like mine, and black besides. I ran between them and hid in the car."

"Maybe she wanted to be sure we knew that we had been dealt a few handicaps, too. Hitting you with being fat; hitting me with tales about my grandmother." Turning the car down toward the clear Weser, I, too, was unsettled by Queen Esther's fragments of truth. "I may not know what I'm getting into, putting her on the show. The day she tells the grandfathers exactly how it is, we'll be in for trouble."

"It nearly drove me crazy to watch that chocolate cake disappear down her gullet. I must have looked that way at ten, as if I were a goose being force-fed for pâté."

To be parked on the dirt road waiting for the shaggy goats to climb the rise into the tick-clinging grasses seemed a bad hiatus in a long day. Hurried, I had not had time to make atonement at Ybarra's eyeless niche or shoo his white cat into the late afternoon.

My mind, still on Grandmother after Jane Brown's tales, brought old scenes between me and the massed herd before me. Whatever drudgery those German women had accepted as their due, they had known when and where to draw battle lines. They knew how to slam doors.

I remembered my first encounter with that defensive retort at which Grandmother excelled.

Usually, when I ate with her, she would float me a piece of buttered bread in a crockery bowl filled with warm milk, a soothing sop for a little girl to spoon and swallow, while she snapped green beans and shelled corn for succotash, and set aside the next day's bread to rise. If my eyelids drooped with the warmth of her hot cook stove, she would add a forbidden taste of coffee to the sweetened milk, a gentle treat from her own girlhood.

On my tenth birthday, however, she greeted me in Sunday hat and dress. I was to accompany her to town.

I can still picture every detail of the Princess Sophie,

that grand hotel where visitors came to stay when they vacationed in Prince Solms, taking their health at the famed Sophie Springs. For townspeople it was a favorite place to meet for an afternoon sweet, under crystal chandeliers in a red-walled Victorian dining room. Now torn down, in memory it remains the most elegant hotel I have ever seen.

An old German waiter presented us with large, stiff menus, written in the language I could not read. I, in brown dress with white collar, was allowed to order their specialty: molded vanilla-bean ice cream, shaped into a horse's head.

Just as I took the first creamy bite from the tall-stemmed silver dish, Grandmother pushed back her chair. "There is no excuse to prepare this from powdered milk and powdered sugar. This is not wartime." Gathered to her full height, she pulled me to my feet. "They have put something over on us." On our way out she complained in person to the manager. "We are not immigrants, as you can see." As she swept out she slammed the front door of the hotel, shaking its curtained leaded glass, jarring each startled patron within.

Back home, we had bread and milk.

Arriving at the cabin first, I turned back the aqua sheets, plumped up the lime plaid pillows—but could not undress.

Sterling, finding me in the bedroom, was ecstatic. "Hey, that's great." He gave me an eager kiss as he felt for a breast. "We could get right to it?"

I stalled. "In a little bit, Sterling. I just got here. Let's have our drink. Tell me about the boys—"

He flashed contrition. "I didn't mean to rush." When he

brought the scotch I was down at the far end of the green fish-floating couch. Keeping his distance, he began the weekly saga. "That Alfred, everything he touches goes wrong. He wrecked the car. Did I tell you?"

"No." Good Alfred.

"His mother's brand-new Olds. He had a bunch of kids with him at the time. They ran into a school bus. So there may be a suit with the city. Which puts me in an awkward spot. In hot water, you could say. His mother thinks the best thing to do with him is to get him a summer job and make him show some responsibility. But I don't know. You can lead a horse to water—" The mayor's face melted into its saggy introspection. Bags crept surreptitiously under his eyes; his smile lines faded into a haggard frown. "He can't do anything right." He was reminded once again that the world was not easy on younger sons. Remembering his own past, he sighed and loosened his tie.

"And Clarence?"

He made the appearance of brightening. "He got accepted at Vanderbilt just like that. Strictly on the basis of his scores. He didn't even have to interview although he plans to anyway. Since he makes a first-class first impression."

"But that takes its toll, too."

"What? I guess so." He moved across the couch close enough to put a hand on my knee. "What do you say we go on back? We can take it nice and slow." He did not need me to remind him of reality; rather he was here to drop his body into some fantasy safe from scrutiny. "When I saw the bed pulled back, I sure got excited. I wish you had got in it for me. Remember, you did that in the hotel room? It really turned me on to see you out of your clothes like that in the bed by yourself."

When we were undressed he shut his eyes and murmured, "Is it exciting for you, by yourself like that?" Guiding me, he whispered, "Tell me, sweetheart, when you're alone do you fool with yourself? Will you show me sometime how you do it?"

Afterward, I huddled down at the other end of the couch, waiting for a second drink. Sterling, sensing that I was not my old self, tried his hand at courting. "Do you know what? I've been working out a big surprise for you, sort of for our anniversary."

"Robin guano season has passed."

"That isn't what I had in mind." He looked hurt.

"What could be finer than those recycled lagustrum berries?"

He edged close and slipped an arm around my bare shoulder. "How about a weekend in a hotel? Remember how you get off to sleeping together? This time we'll have two nights with no interference. San Antonio's hosting a meeting of the Big City Mayors, so it'll be strictly legitimate for me to be at the hotel. Plus, it just so happens that it's also the wife's annual South Texas weekend with the girls. A dozen of them go across the border to shop every year; though, just between you and me, I think they go down mostly for the margaritas. What do you say?"

"When?"

"Middle of next week. Wednesday through Friday. The conference will end with the Friday prayer breakfast."

"Very fitting." I moved the ice around in my glass. "My friend Minna, the newswoman from Washington, is going over Wednesday to be on the 'High Noon' show. I'm going with her."

"Terrific. Then you'll be there anyway. A good excuse."

"You don't understand. I'm driving her over; I have to drive her back."

"Can't she handle that by herself?"

"How? Ride the bus?"

"Take her home and come on back." He massaged my thigh. "Look, sweetheart, I've got this all set up for us."

"I'll see." It was time to get dressed. It was beginning to dim outside the aqua sea-shelled curtains. The drive back seemed long. The thought of a drive another day, foolish.

The mayor, interpreting my hedging as success, got up in good spirits. "Don't forget your black-lace nightie."

Parked back on the dirt road, eating my sandwich from home, hearing far off the hoofs of the goats, I thought of Grandmother. I needed to take lessons from the covert ways a German woman was allowed to rebuff her man. I needed to learn how to tell the mayor he was on the wrong side of my life.

I remembered a story about Grandmother and the snakes. Her copper wash kettle shared a dirt-floored outbuilding with stored grains and smoked hams from slaughtered hogs. This shed served also as a discreet spot for her morning smoke. One day, settled on the edge of the kettle to moisten an end paper around a dab of tobacco from the pouch tied under her skirt, she came roaring back outside, hollering for the field hands. Inside the copper pot, curled tight as a ball of twine, were twenty-two rattlesnakes who had come in from the fields to feed on the mice, who, in turn, had crawled between the planks of the shed to gnaw into the sacks of cracked corn. Grandfather and his brother had killed them with a hoe.

The whispered story I overheard from the young uncles was that for the four months it took to build her a separate washhouse with a board floor and white walls, Grandfather still had his clothes scrubbed clean daily, and still got his hogshead cheese and supper dumplings, but he no longer received the favors of the marriage bed. In silent retribution, Grandmother had nightly wrapped the bed-sheet tight as a shroud around her.

But times have changed. Back then a woman might twist herself in a sheet to strike a bargain, for then husband and wife were bound together by law, economics, habit, and the assumption of a common bed.

But in the present, the same rules would not apply. Sterling, upon finding me wound mummy fashion, would say, "Is that sexy for you, tied up like that, sweetheart?"

Now, honking a signal to the far-off goats in the twilight, I considered that Grandmother would take a dim view of my continued rendezvous with the mayor. Seeing it through her eyes: I was reappearing weekly at the Princess Sophie dining room to be served the same ice cream made of powdered milk and powdered sugar, was weekly cutting my spoon into the same soft white mold, shaped like a horse's ass.

EIGHT

Re-enter the Prince

On Good Friday, I was bringing my listeners a preview of San Antonio's most lavish social event, Fiesta. A seven-day-and-night affair, it is as historic as the city's Alamo. Hotel rooms, from which to view its Battle of the Flowers parade, are booked years in advance. Its parties are carefully graded, in the unspoken manner of high society, according to which men's order sponsors them and which old families attend. My intention was to make all the Austin gentry, who drive over annually to such lesser events as beer and bratwurst at Beethoven Hall or the Fiesta Flambeau, feel that they were insiders; the true insiders, of course, would not be tuning in to Pasture Radio during the two crescendo-building weeks before the event.

I would have liked to interview Fiesta's queen, she who is unveiled to gasps of surprise in her spectacular bejeweled and embroidered gown and robe at the cherished (but not exclusive) Coronation Ball; she who later glides with her attendants—Ledas on swans—down the winding river in the heart of town.

I would have liked to unfold for my listeners what was in the heart of such a queen, burdened with fifty pounds of velvet, lace, and brilliants; burdened also with the knowledge that the crown on her head cost her fine old family fifty thousand dollars. "How does it feel, that pressure, that heritage?" I would have asked her. But whereas on television her answer would not matter—as we could see into the heart of her, perspiring, aspiring, roseate, and awed—on radio something would be shattered at her faint voice replying, "Gee, it's really neat, you know?"

So, instead, our guest was Fiesta's Mistress of the Wardrobe, that grand dame who designs—in secret sessions with mamas, sorority sisters, and old aunties about color preferences, family legends, and favorite things—the special costumes for the queen, princess, and each of the duchesses. Her role here was to titillate our audience with anecdotes from the Sketch Party at which each girl is presented a secret advance painting of her dress, train, headpiece, and hand piece.

Had I followed my logic in presenting the engineer who actually dumped the green dye in the river, I would have invited one of the eight seamstresses who work as handmaidens to the five dressmakers who carry out the designs of the wardrobe mistress. But I could think of nothing to ask them. "Do your eyes go red from sewing on ten thousand seed pearls the size of sand grains?" I feared that, nervous, and at a loss, I would lapse into ultimate probings: "Are you spinning flax into gold?" "Are you setting stones or building a cathedral?"

The mistress had arrived, despite instructions not to, with a dozen sketches of her garments, which, as I had pointed out on the phone, our fans were not going to be able to see. Composed and waiting on the other side of the glass booth, she wore one of those coatsuits that declare themselves to be costly. Not a Paris collection model which could often by the unknowing be mistaken for something your Vietnamese seamstress had produced, but a suit about which there could be no mistake that it was or could have been a Geoffrey Beene, and did, or could have, cost seven hundred dollars. It was a caramel and tan houndstooth checked skirt and flaring jacket of a slick wool blend with a matching silk shirt of the same caramel and tan, that in narrow stripes. The blouse's large bow spilled loosely over the covered coat buttons, to show that the checks and stripes were made to go together. Her hair, tinted caramel, seemed to come from the same dyer, as did her tortoise eyeglasses and lizard shoes. Very effective: she looked identical to those newspaper pictures of women who have just been elected national presidents of voluntary organizations. A well-co-ordinated co-ordinator.

On the air she told well-assembled vignettes. She described the appearance of a dozen peacocks at the childhood Easter egg hunt of one of last year's duchesses; hence the special significance on her gown of the spreading peacock done in seven shades of green and violet baguettes and sequins.

As we described the gown in detail, Otto got the phone. "Tex-Czech," he mouthed to me, beaming.

I'm not sure what happened to the egg hunt or that green bird. For all I can remember of the rest of the interview, the mistress eventually prevailed, and flashed her sketches to the blind mike. At some point I eased her off the air with Delbert McClinton's swinging ode to "Ruby Louise."

"Hi," I said into the receiver.

"I'm going to Sophienburg tomorrow for the Easter Eve fires."

"Wending your way?"

A pause. "Actually, I am."

"You're letting me invite myself along?"

"If you want to."

"Is it my turn to bring the peanut butter and jelly?"

"I think we can do better this time. Don't the Germans set out their sausage in the streets at these things?"

"We could find out."

"I'd like to get up there while it's still light."

"I'd like to go, Billy Wayne."

"How about four o'clock?"

"An agreeable time."

"I'll come by your place." Showing at least that he remembered he had been under the lagustrum before.

I cradled the phone and laid my face on the pile of Fiesta notes.

"They don't move fast, do they?" Otto plugged in a public service spot prior to his daily bad news of no rain in sight.

"They don't."

Later, when our guest had gone, I sat on the table in the control room, my blue-jeaned knees pulled tight to my chest. "Maybe he only comes up every season, for air."

"You have to get him up to your place, then things will go faster."

"He's been to my place." I rocked back and forth. "Brought his string with him. It didn't move things along at all."

"He's been thinking about it," Otto pronounced, hooking his thumbs through his suspenders.

"What's he been thinking?"

"Sometimes I think: that woman is going to be trouble. Sometimes I think: that woman is all right."

"What keeps you from calling back?"

"When the same woman is both things."

"That's no help."

"It's the second phone call which counts."

"We'll see."

"It vill be a dry spell for the grandfathers." Otto, back into his role, picked up on the last sound of the song.

The star-shaped, gingerbread town of Sophienburg had turned itself into a gay sidewalk festival to commemorate its past.

But Gruene and I were poor tourists. We both worked without being able to help it: he, swinging his eyes in all directions to seek revelations of ancient symbols and old folklore beneath the beneficence of smiling women selling apricot kolache to would-be lovers; I, catching snatches of conversations to suit the Ear. (A pudgy woman says to her pudgy mate, "You do, too, waddle. Even your own mother says it. You have a very distinct waddle.")

Waiting for the writer on the stairs outside my garage apartment, I had been reminded of a fairy tale in which one sister stands on the parapet waiting for the prince to appear while the other, the heroine, calls repeatedly from within, "Sister Anne, sister Anne, do you see him coming?" It brought back to me the whole female thing of waiting for *his* call or *his* arrival. I couldn't even recall in the story why the one who loved the prince was not the one who strained her eyes for the first glimpse of him on the horizon. Maybe she could not endure the absence of horse's hoofs sending dust into the air.

I had dressed for him in Easter colors: a purple linen skirt, a sheer yellow cotton blouse gathered full below a square neckline, pink ceramic earrings clasped under the edge of just-washed hair.

He had stepped from his shiny Ford in another version of cowboy: just-purchased khaki jeans, stiff white shirt.

It was hard to tell how it felt to see him again. My body reacted below the level of saying; it stopped me still at the top of the stairs. Maybe that was why the princess herself had not waited at the window—she stood rooted within by the remembrance of him.

Now, making the sidewalk rounds, we tried to mingle with the crowd. At first we held hands, but then, as it was not casual, we let go. We tried eating chewy gummy sweets, sold beneath flapping pink and white buntings, along with those pecan and coconut frosted German chocolate cakes stuffed with the fortunetelling promises of tin thimbles, ships, babies, and rings.

We admired the window of a hardware store featuring a model which reconstructed the first immigrations to this city of five valleys; and a museum display of mannequins re-creating a turn-of-the-century ball—white gowns and piled hair waltzing with mustaches and waistcoats.

For what seemed an hour we poked around in the lobby of the Admiral Nimitz Hotel wandering among its display of Second World War weaponry: Nazi and Allied uniforms, helmets, hand grenades, warheads, shards of ships and tanks, swords, medals, land mines, intricate reconstructions of naval battles.

"I can't believe they have this here," I said. "When you think that these Germans fought on the wrong side of every war; against the South in the Civil War, sympathizing with the old country in the World Wars. You'd think from this that they had been heroes every time."

"They don't admit to being losers."

"Why aren't we taking lessons?"

Across an autographed copy of the admiral as a youth, Gruene caught my arm. "For God's sake let's get out of here."

We found a dark, noisy *Wursthalle* where the polkas poured forth as fast as Michelob on tap.

It was then, for the first time taking my eyes from his face, that I saw the shoes. On his feet, instead of the shiny cowboy boots, were old, brown, scuffed, lace-up shoes with runover heels.

"What happened to your boots?"

"I left them on the porch at the ranch and something carried them off in the night."

"Your dog?"

"Not him. He would bring them inside." He looked down. "These are the only other pair I had. When I realized I would have to wear them, I nearly didn't come. I almost called you. I can't get out of my mind where they used to walk."

"Sooner or later you're going to have to admit you weren't born one afternoon at Dobie's ranch."

"I had planned on later. A lot later."

"What's in your sack?" I indicated a brown paper bag he had lugged along with him. "You promised no sandwiches."

"Easter eggs."

"Hand dyed of course."

"I thought I might want them, at the Fires."

"If your mind is on that, what are we doing in here listening to the polkas?"

"I ask you to these things," he said, "Spreewald and the Fires, and then I don't seem able to do justice by you or them. My mind can't seem to stay either on you or on their ancient rituals. I try to do both at once and end by doing neither."

"You're the one who said two things were possible at once."

"Not these."

"I'm not in your room, Billy."

"It may be I put you there."

"Don't blame me."

We drank two more rounds as a fat-bellied man played his fat-bellied fiddle. By then my sandals rested against his old shoes under the table, and he held my purple knees tight between his.

"I didn't call you," he said, "because I couldn't figure out how to work and see you both. I got home from that trip to see the church at Spreewald with no notes at all. I couldn't even envision the inside of it, when I shut my eyes. I had to go back, the next week, alone."

"I didn't call you either. Figuring I could make do without someone who preferred to sleep with his dog and jerk off with some Italian woman spreading it out in his head."

"It wasn't preference. You know that. It was the only way I could keep my mind on my work. Besides, how is that, what you said, any different from you with the mayor?"

"He shows me these pictures of his sons—"

"Still?"

"Still."

"You're his Italian in a satin slip."

"Maybe."

"Seeing me didn't make any difference then?"

"I didn't say that. It did. It made it harder for me to be alone in my blue walls. A lot of things."

"Would you have seen him again, if I had come back?"

"You can't lay claim, Billy, because you tied your string in my bed one time. But, yes, all right, I might have seen him anyway."

"Why?"

"Because I would not have wanted to count too much on you. To count on a person changes things."

"Am I not to count on this?"

"Not if you let it get between you and your work."

"It's not your showing your bathing-suit line; I know

you've done that before. It's the level he puts it on; I don't want it to be that way with us."

"So it's been no way at all."

He let that stand. Finally, in the din of music and the smell of beer, he took hold of my arm. "What is it you are afraid of being changed into, Avery?"

"Mama. Anyone's. The hausfrau of Papa. Anyone's."

"Yes, that's the danger. That's one reason I hold back."

"What are you saying, then? That there are no alternatives to nookie with a public official and making pfeffernuss cookies in the kitchen?"

"If I knew alternatives I might be offering them."

"What are you offering?"

"Another chance to tag along while I research the Wends." I felt his legs tighten on each side of mine.

"Which I'm confusing."

"I didn't say it was your fault."

"It isn't. I'm not a siren seeking to wreck your ship. I'm not competing with your book. I'm a Swede used to sending words out into the air come to see why you want to anchor yours to paper."

"Let's go try it, then. It's time." He left the waitress a tip and in one motion slid his hand down my yellow shirt to my purple hips.

"You're afraid of being changed, too." I told him at the door as we hit the hot, slanting, disappearing sun.

"Yes. Back into the guy who wore these shoes."

At the County Fairgrounds we climbed the bleachers through the hundreds of grandfathers and grandmothers and mamas and papas and cousins and neighbors of the stars of the show. Women with arms like rising loaves, in tucked, flowered Sunday dresses, had pinned their hair into sausage curls; narrow-chested, hatted men in bow ties had got their necks shaved in old-country haircuts. All settled their bulk to wait for that first glimpse of a ringleted daughter or a bespectacled son. A fat woman shoved a handkerchief between her ample breasts. "Our Rosalie will be a beauty, won't she, Oskar? Won't she?" A stringy little man turned to his wife. "Anna, our Henry will make a fine settler, hey, Anna?"

At first it seemed the same as any performance of local talent, put on not for its merits but to give each child a brief instant in the limelight. The sort of bumbling show, unbelievable in its duration, bearable only for that moment when your own offspring makes an entrance.

While six-foot bundles of twigs were set in place to represent hilltops, an announcer told us that directly or indirectly seven hundred people had made tonight's show possible. Seventy-five of them were recognized by name and applauded.

While choir directors, scoutmasters, homeroom teachers, and lodge members readied the vast cast beneath the stands, and Gruene vanished into his story, I read the official program:

Scene One: The Indians (played by Junior Boys from the Missionary Baptist Church)
Scene Two: The Colonists (played by Hermann Sons' Lodge members' sons)
Scene Three: Birth of the Easter Fires: A Pioneer Mother tells the Children, who are afraid of the Indian fires on the

hills, that it is only the Rabbit boiling eggs (Mother played by Mrs. Woodrow "Woody" Wooten. Children played by Mrs. Hans Jessie Gunter's kindergarten class)

Scene Four: Wildflowers are gathered into nests (played by Sophienburg Brownie Scout Troop ♯3)

Scene Five: Rabbit, his Wife, and the Little Bunnies dye eggs (played by Dr. and Mrs. Charles "Chuck" Mueller and the little Muellers)

Scene Six: Grand Finale. Peace Treaty between Colonists and Indians. Children find nests in which Rabbit and Bunnies have placed Easter eggs (Entire cast)

It was now pitch dark as the Indians assembled behind the faggots out of sight and the stout German boys portraying the colonists came onto the field from behind a parked truck.

Small children, played by smaller children, gathered around their mother as a bevy of wildflowers in homemade violet petals waltzed on in a giggling entrance.

The only jarring notes seemed typical German ironies: that the redmen were played by blacks; that the countrymen huddled around fasces.

Then, as the Indians lit the bonfires with torches, sending flames shooting into the air, the Rabbit—sinister and white—entered from the left.

I reached for Gruene. Nothing, of course, was what it had seemed. Beneath the garbled story of the bunnies and the nests and the comforted children, old myths held sway.

For the first time I saw it through his eyes, as if a spell has been cast; or as if, behind an innocent street scene on the front of the stage, the hero and villain push their way through the crowd, as the music mounts, to enact their fateful duel.

This, then, was what he strained his hazel eyes to see beneath the flax and berries, the cross and sword, the one God and the many, this awesome mix of Christian and heathen that reached as far back in our pasts as dimmest legend.

In the silence of the grand finale—with the redmen and immigrants at peace and the children happy with their Easter eggs, and the high school band booming the *Deutschland* march—the Rabbit (that white-robed clansman) lit a ten-foot gas-soaked cross.

I shuddered, as did Gruene next to me. For us the pyre echoed Judas burned at the Wends' stake, a cannibalistic Indian roasting a settler, lynchings in the ancient South, and Jesus, risen on a blazing crucifix.

As if in answering signal, the dark hills circling us burst into flame.

"Gruene, look." We sat motionless as five giant bonfires ringed us in fire.

By the time we got through the crowds down into the dirt arena, the show was over; the Rabbit in Gethsemane had discarded his disguise. All that was left were aromatic clumps of singed cedar branches, and the smoldering embers into which Gruene dropped his archaic blood-red eggs.

"The cross—" I said.

"I know."

"The Rabbit—"

"It was all there, wasn't it?"

At the car he said, "I want to see the Fires."

"I know a road up that hill; it leads to a park."

"Let's hurry then. I want to get there before they go out."

But as we crawled along in a caravan of a thousand blinking headlights, it began to rain. At first a sprinkle; by the time we reached the side road which climbed steeply up the nearest hill, it had begun to pour.

"Will this put them out?"

Gruene shook his head. "I think they soak the wood in gasoline."

Alone on a shadowy back road we spun gravel as we traversed steep switchbacks which ended at a locked park gate. On the rise above us a crackling blaze spit steam back at the rain. Its attendants, dark as hangmen, stood silhouetted on either side—sentinels. I wondered if they watched us.

Shutting off the motor, Gruene looked out the blurred windshield.

It was good finally to be alone with him, and I wanted badly the feel of him, the solid, concrete, immediate presence to counteract the layered ghosts of old burnings from other centuries that we had seen. "What does the fire mean?" I asked, as he made no move to close the space between us.

"Death. All cultures tell of fertility and death. It's all the same, old rites or modern ones, they can't bring hope without a warning."

"I found it terrifying."

"That's what I came to see." He squinted through the rain to the hill above us.

Wanting him, I put his hand on the front of my yellow blouse.

He pulled me to him. "It was good to have you along."

I slid my hand along his khaki pants. "I have cheese and gin at the apartment."

But he didn't answer. Instead he stroked my blouse awhile and then pushed his hand up under it, until, with his help, I took it off. In the half light he pulled his shirt off, too, becoming again the cowboy whose tan stopped at the neck.

Touching his pale chest, I remembered aloud, "I once slept with a man with a hairy belly."

"Was that good?"

"The belly? Yes."

"Those things get mixed together. The only woman I ever knew with huge breasts had tumbleweeds of black hair under her arms and in her crotch. I associate the two."

"Was that good?"

"Not at the time. Sometimes it is to remember."

"What about the woman who stayed with you? The grand finale every night."

"She was sort of cherry colored. Her mouth and hair. I don't know. Long legs."

Aware of my bare top, I imagined him telling someone down the road about the Swede with the thin chest and the wide thighs and the albino hair.

"Don't," he said, touching me. "Don't project."

"How can you tell?"

"Because I was doing it myself."

He reached up under my skirt as he kissed my head back

against the seat. "It's been a long time since I made it in a car."

"We can go home—"

"I want it here. Would you mind the ground?"

"Come around and help me out."

Under heavy tree limbs, he smoothed a place on the gravel shoulder. Pulling me from the car he took off my purple skirt and underpants, and spread his tan jeans for me to lie on. "Do you want something under your head?"

"Your brown shoe."

On his knees he said, "I thought of this a lot."

"So did I."

Then he began to love me on the rocky ground, shielding me from the dripping leaves with his bare back, until we were drenched, and he had skinned his elbows, and I had bruised my back, and we had flung out our breaths, losing our selves.

Back in the car we ran the motor for a little heat.

"I missed that," I said.

"When?"

I thought it out. "Mostly by myself. When I'm with other people, at the studio or at Grandfather's, then I am concentrating on what's happening, on understanding what is true in what I hear and see. You made it harder to make sense of things alone; you reminded me of a time I had forgotten."

"Do you know what's happening now?"

"We did it in the rain."

"More than that."

"What is more than that?"

His face widened happily. "Nothing is more. Some things are in addition."

"What?"

"Loving."

"That is counting on someone." I put my mouth against his, to silence him. "Show me how to do it in a car."

"Let me come around and get in on that side. Where there's no steering wheel."

As I waited in the rain he climbed in and pulled me to him. Silently I grabbed his hair and put my elbows on his shoulder. Then, as he guided, I lowered myself on him and went a little wild: thinking that this was what I had been looking for when I went off to that green college town. Thinking that it was lovely to know at last what it was all about.

As I grew still, my cheek against his, content, the night went suddenly dark as the inside of a sooty mine.

"Damn," he said. "The fire went out."

NINE

The Seeing Eye

Minna wore the wrong clothes for television. Arriving in black pants, and a top of black and white geometric checks, she threw the hostess of "High Noon" into a frenzy.

"I should have told you what to wear. I thought someone from the East would know." Terry Lynn Taylor waved her arms. "Never mind, they tell me our new cameras can handle black and white now, which they couldn't used to do. We all still wear pastels." For today's show the brisk redhead had on a tan knit dress with a knotted green scarf at the neck which matched her bright green beads. "I have a whole wardrobe of scarves," she confided, "and a whole drawer full of color co-ordinated jewelry. I try not to repeat what I wear for a month. They expect variety;

look at Barbara Walters. But if I change what's at the neckline, then it looks like a different dress. I wear a lot of interchangeable separates. If you worked around TV you'd catch on."

"I'm in the newspaper business," Minna retorted. "Black and white and read all over." She held a cigarette between painted nails.

"Ha, ha." Terry Lynn did a quick once-over of her visitor and then, after offering us cups of tepid coffee, she led us into her territory: a large TV studio with a mock living room which was her stage. As she moved us along she gave us the rundown. "When I have a celebrity, someone like Paul Newman, say, then he sits up with me during the entire hour, sort of a co-host. But mostly we put our guests over there." She gestured to a row of chairs off camera. "Where you'll be. Then we call them on when it's their turn. Your first part comes on after the second commercial. You have two six-minute spots. Then, besides my special guests, I have a public service feature which, today, is a representative of the San Antonio African Violet Association. Sometimes, I might have two shorter public service features, when there are several things of interest to the viewers. If you had been here yesterday you could have seen the end of my ecology series. I like to do a weekly series sometimes during the year; last year I did a feature on adoptable children, and the year before we did a guide to free recreation. It keeps up some interest, you know, gives some continuity."

She showed Minna to a chair near a woman I presumed to be the African Violet, beside a man in a plaid suit who waved at Terry to let her know he was there.

"Honey," she said to me, having forgotten my name, "you want to wait over there by the wall for your friend? Or you can grab a quick Danish downstairs."

What I really wanted to do, of course, was get to the heart or the brain of that other medium that could bring you the smile of Fiesta's queen or the wink of the St. Patrick's Day midgets. I wanted to see the source of the Eye. "I thought I might mosey around," I told her. "Go look at the machines. Would that be all right?"

Terry looked blank. "What do you mean, machines? Like the TCR?"

"Right. The TCR." I imagined the Wizard of Oz, with me being led down the halls of the palace to find the central being enthroned and bathed in emerald light, an ordinary mastermind, the TCR. A seductive vision.

"Well, if you head out that way, you'll find the control room. Check with the VE, honey, that's video engineer."

"Wonderful."

Once within the outer corridors of what appeared to be a protracted maze, I followed young men in tight trousers and trailed young women bearing clipboards until, turning into a smaller square, I came upon an intent man whose eyes appeared accustomed to the interior's bottled light. Busily his fingers counted some wavelength. He worked, apparently, on the brain.

"Could you take me to the TCR?"

He glanced up, puzzled. "It's over there, miss."

"I don't know what it is."

"The tape cartridge recorder? It's over there. You don't work around here, do you?"

"I want to know how you get pictures from in here to

out there. I don't understand television. I work in radio. I don't understand how my friend's face is going to be in all those kitchens with the women eating tuna salad."

"You have to understand physics, lady."

"I don't, if you do."

Reluctantly he indicated a nearby wide slick tape, which was being swallowed on its side like a rabbit into a boa constrictor.

"What is it doing?"

He shook his head in frustration. I peered at him. He was the kind of man, who, no matter how trained and promoted, hears with his hands. He was the same as the mechanic where I took the Datsun; all the time we stood and talked carburetors and distributors, his grease-caked hands twitched. This slightly squinting man was the same: as we talked he worked his hands in reflex, almost in imitation of the reeling reel. "I'll tell you what I know, and you can go from there. I know that a player piano has holes in its paper tapes and that when those holes strike the tiny metal teeth it plays a tune."

"Okay. On video the magnetic lines induce a voltage in a coil, then the four heads on the wheel hit it vertically, and you get a picture."

"How do the wheels translate? How do they read dots? Do they write out dots the way a newspaper does?"

He nodded and pointed above the tape swallower. "That screen up there scans back and forth five hundred and twenty-five times from top to bottom and fills in the image from the top down."

I thought of tombstone rubbings, and the waxy pages you rubbed a pencil on to bring out an image.

"You have to know physics," he repeated. "The amplitude gives you brightness and the frequency gives you the picture segments." He cracked his knuckles.

"How does it move from one image to the next?" In my head I flipped the pages of Big-Little books, watching the tiny figures run and jump and play ball.

"Phosphorus keeps it illuminated as it moves to a new frame."

"Then you use the human eye as well?" How fine. One eye creates another. What a marvel. Enough of brain; I was ready for the heart. "Show me the cameras."

Glancing at his machine, he shut off the whirring boa and led me down another canal around a corner into the smallest room of all. The ventricle of the heart.

"This is a film camera. They're about out of style now, since we got video tape and cartridges."

"Where is the camera looking?" I peered into a strange box that saw only into a large box in which mirrors were raised and lowered to focus it onto the slides of film being shown it by projectors. It could see nothing that was not put before it; it was a camera which took pictures only of pictures. "My God," I gasped in revelation. "It's blind; this is the true Mole."

Amazing maze; amazing place. Amazing revelations of electronic anatomy like a peek into the illustrations of the health book. It was wholly unexpected: to fall in love at first sight with television.

I patted the box whose inside was dark as cat-black velvet. What a fine box. What an instructive man; I patted him, too. "My friend is going to be out there, phosphorescent dots. I have to go."

136

"She's on 'High Noon'?"

"Appearing as black and white on living color."

By the stage set Terry Lynn and Minna chewed the fat, making one another highly anxious, waiting for the count-down.

"How did you happen to get into TV?" Minna asked. "I've always been fascinated by it." She stared idly around the studio, her face denying her words.

"You mean in the first place? I got into it early on, I'll say that, before they invented all the radio-television-film degrees they have today. I was an army widow, second time around. When the first one went—you probably don't know how it was then, but he was a major with a wartime commission and looked straight out of the movies—I got a job in a health spa. They even made me a manager, said I had more sense than their college graduates even though I didn't have a high school diploma. But I had sense enough to know you can't stay in a place like that indefinitely; they only want you while you're young and your butt is high.

"So by the time the second one smoked himself to death, another military type—this one with a permanent commis-sion, who had to sit up in the chair all night at the last to breathe—I had my credentials. I had tried it out in St. Louis, and I moved right into it in San Antonio. If you want the truth, the station manager had been trying to get into my pants for a year before I applied for my present job." She studied her nails. It was too familiar to dwell on, the tactics of survival.

Something about her was reminiscent of old forties

movies: the hint of shoulder pads, the suggestion of a pompadour, the bright-coated mouth. She was waiting for the boys to come home again. What a fine movie for her to be in: San Antonio, that museum of the military.

On cue she and her male weather-and-newsman took their places in easy chairs on each side of a formica coffee table, its vase of permanent flowers in the same brassy shades as the oil painting behind them. As he smoothed his sprayed, razor-cut hair, Terry Lynn began, "Welcome to 'High Noon,' everybody. We have a lot of excitement here today, including a lady reporter all the way from Washington, D.C., and all our regular fun and public service features."

Leaning against the wall directly facing Terry, I became the Seeing Eye, moving in, zooming in, as Camera Number Two, for a close-up of our hostess.

The possibilities of my new sense were limitless. I longed to pan for a shot of the newscaster's hair, to fill the screen with its lacquered immobility. Or to blow up Terry's green beads and crepy neck until all the viewer could see was the motion of her throat as she mouthed unseen words. Electrifying images possible to vision. It felt so grand: to *see*.

When Minna took her place for her first six minutes, I shifted her black and white diamonds into a magnetic blur that raised the voltage and entranced the audience. Cutting to her full view, I watched her do the tricks of this video as if born to it. All the devices which were weakness on the Ear she practiced as strength—the pause, the hover, the fidget, the delay.

As long as Minna raised her thin-plucked brows, laughed

slightly, hunted for an answer, the camera, and therefore the viewer, was hers. Terry Lynn sat helpless until a reply came forth.

"What brings you down our way, Miss Raabe?" Terry did not use first names; guests received word to call her Mrs. Taylor on the show.

"Well." Minna stretched her face into a knowing smile as she expanded her visibility. "You know it's the congressman's home district . . ."

Terry Lynn sat up straight to field this unexpected reply. "Are you doing a report on Congressman Vlasig, then?"

"Oh no." Minna unfurled innuendo. "No, no. We're just friends. People always misunderstand us. We're just friends." She made a shrugging gesture as if denying an onslaught of rumor. "We're from the same home town, so people always . . . Truly, it just sort of evolved." She smiled warmly at my widened aperture.

Terry Lynn made a fast move to change the subject. "I believe you mentioned that you were down here to do a story?"

"Oh, yes, I am." Minna turned her face toward mine to be sure that I, as Camera Two, caught it all. "Yes, I'm doing an article on penile implants—"

Terry Lynn flashed a frozen smile. Not quite sure she'd heard right, but too smart by far to pursue it, she cut Minna off at the pass. "And that's all the time we have for Miss Raabe for now, but we'll be back with more . . ."

The suited man turned out to be the garden club representative; the woman was his wife. Their six minutes brought gardeners everywhere time and place and hours of the upcoming show. They reminded me of the fans at football games who discover they are on camera and, tickled, frantically wave to their mothers in Abilene.

In her last six minutes, Minna, having recanted and assumed a solemn air, gave straight talk about the perils of a "lady" in the male world of investigative reporters. Somewhat mollified, Terry Lynn Taylor walked us to the elevator after the show.

"How come," Minna asked idly, "you had the African Violet's wife come along?"

"When they told me the club's representative was a man, I didn't want my viewers to get any kind of wrong idea. You have to be careful that you don't create the wrong impression with something like a man growing flowers."

Minna looked at her blandly. "Or a woman throwing a softball?"

Terry tried in vain to follow the thread. "We don't usually get into athletics since we're a noon show. Unless a pro ballplayer or someone is in town. Then we let him co-host the show."

In the car Minna flung her head back against the seat. "What a weirdo, that woman. I should have called to ask her the bead color for the day. Out of touch as I am, I believed that the rule that you couldn't wear black and white on the screen was twenty years out of date."

I confessed, "I fell in love with it. Television is the ultimate invasion of privacy. The medium for the true voyeur. If I'd been Camera Two I'd have done a close-up of the Violet's wife tugging at her girdle just before they came on camera. Then moved up from her fanny and hands to the look she shot her husband as they went on the air. All those wordless humanities that radio misses. I'd have swallowed Terry Lynn's face with the screen when you shot her the implants so that all we saw was her gaping mouth change slowly into the super smile."

"I was going to tell her I went down to Houston to monitor the nocturnal tumescence, and check out the cylindrical silicone prostheses. Very phallic. I talked to an actual recipient: 'As far as sexual activities, I have no problem there.' Talked to the urologist who dreamed it up: 'I think our social attitudes in the past were such that patients would have been too humiliated to come in. Too closely tied to a man's virility.' The one I really wanted to see, the engineer who did all the work of figuring it out, was back in Minnesota. My boss turned on like a light when I called the story in; said the capital was full of takers."

"Think what you did for Willy's image."

"Now he owes us both a favor." She shifted complacently in her seat. "How did it go Saturday with the writer?"

"I put his fire out."

"That bad?"

"No, nice. I expect to hear from him again, probably at Halloween. There are a lot of superstitions we can look into. Witches we can burn; black magic to perform."

"I think I'll ask about the mayor instead. At least I won't get an ambiguous answer."

"Sterling?" Heading down the highway from San Antonio as fast as I could go, ten miles over the speed limit, I began to laugh. Amazed that I had honestly forgotten his honor. All thought of wriggling in a hotel room had fled when I encountered the intoxicating Eye. "As a matter of fact he is, at this very moment, waiting for me in a hotel room, having slipped away from the other Big City Mayors who, doubtless, have also slipped away to their afternoon chippies. Imagine. He will be livid."

"You didn't tell me you were to meet him. What was I supposed to do? Take notes? Do it in tandem?"

"He wears white socks."

"Nothing kinky then."

It must be that with every step we take—eating with Olga Dolle, waiting on the outside stairs for Fords to show, speeding down the freeway—we make a choice. Even with our backs turned and our heads agog with other matters, we are deciding all the time. A reassuring thought for one who has not mastered Grandmother's forthright style.

"I think I finally slammed a door."

TEN

Calling in a Past Debt

Delighted not to be in a hotel room, enacting alienation, groping around on a burgher's body, I lay, instead, on my own blue-spread bed, nude, brushing my hair dry: damp flax, carded by hand.

My mind was still on television and my instant infatuation with sending out multiple images of Minna like moving Xerox copies; her phosphorescent dots reassembling across a thousand lunch tables.

My eyes remembered a dozen pictures once seen and filed which they now offered back to me for my reviewing. There were eighty-year-old twins I had seen, as a child, in a cafeteria: rosy mirror images of one another, in matching pink ruffled dresses, and pink patent pumps, with rouged cheeks and ringleted rabbity hair. Like greedy babies they stole tidbits from one another's plates to stuff into their duplicate pinked and pouting mouths.

From the double image, I went crazy with repetition: a pride of nuns in flying stiff white hats; a tall black basketball team, all dribbling in unison; a gaggle of Girl Scouts. The Masons with their armbands. Their women in the tan fur-tacked coats.

The phone invaded the camera in my head and ground my visions to a blur. "Yes?" I answered, jarred.

"What happened to you?" It was Sterling. Not only had I forgotten our earlier tryst, I had forgotten that he had not.

"I had to drive Minna home. I told you."

"You said you'd work that out. Don't you remember? You said you'd be there. We even talked about you bringing your nightgown and all. You could have called the room at least and not just stood me up. I told you this time it would be in my name, the room. Strictly legitimate. I told you. I don't understand. I waited for you till two o'clock."

"I should have called." I brushed the ends of my hair, turning flax into gold.

"Well, hey, are you there? I can be through tonight by eight. We'll still have two nights and that's the main thing. We're right looking down on the river, see. We can pull the curtains a little and have our drinks. Probably hear a mariachi band, if you like that sort of thing. What do you say? Eight o'clock?"

"I'm not driving back over there again, Sterling."

"What's got into you, anyway? Don't talk like that. Are

you nervous about the hotel? Afraid somebody . . . Look, you want to try the cabin? I could stay until maybe ten. Or, hey, I can skip cocktails altogether and get there by six."

"I don't want to go to the cabin; I don't want to wait on the shaggy goats." At that exact moment a freckle on my thigh began to move, imperceptibly revealing itself as variety number four, the star-backed tick. No matter that I probably got it on the ground after the Easter Fires, it seemed a dread and all too real symbol of all I had hated about the Medina River bank.

"Listen, I don't know what's the matter. I figured you got tied up on the 'High Noon' show and then you had to take your friend home, and that can happen to anybody. But, sweetheart, you're not giving me anything to go on."

"I don't want you to go on." I pinched the head off the clinging trespasser on my leg.

"Don't get highhanded on me, now." The mayor puffed in frustration at this unaccountable breakdown between us.

"Sterling, what you need to do is start scouting for a replacement; the river walk is full of them. I'm retiring, having had enough of lime and aqua." In relief I rolled onto my stomach to brush my tresses toward the floor. "If you want references—"

"Look, I could make trouble, you know. The station manager is a friend of mine. I could put a certain word or two about you and that Mexican you work with in his ear and you'd be out on your ear the next day."

"Ear fetish."

"Listen to me, I know what I'm talking about. I know how to get these things done. Come on, will you come to your senses? I can't stand here on the phone trying to make you listen all afternoon." His voice had stretched to a tight whine.

"Shouldn't stand on it; Mother Bell won't like that." I flung my hairbrush against the wall in sudden fury. "You think threats are going to make me hot in bed? You're out of your mind, Sterling. This is a personal matter between you and me. We're quits. That's got nothing to do with my job at KPAC."

"I just wanted to start you thinking about a few things is all."

"The trouble is, I've already thought of them." I dropped the phone in its cradle. What a bourgeois. Always the Germans do it the same way, always they have only the one weapon: economic reprisal. How could they see it any other way, the petty merchants?

While I considered the ultimate retaliation against his elected honor's petulant threat, I allowed myself the diversion of a warm-up revenge.

I had called the mayor's office only once during our year's alliance, and then only to relay to his secretary the discreet message that I would have to postpone our discussion of a repeat radio interview—not wanting to explain to her the matter of my sore, red throat.

This time I set out to create the impression I had thoughtfully avoided the time before. "May I speak to Sterling Price, please?"

"May I say who's calling?" A honeyed voice poured over the phone.

"This is Avery Krause in Prince Solms."

"The mayor is attending a conference this afternoon. Would you care to leave your number, Miss Krause?"

"Oh, that Sterling. He's always in meetings."

Honey drew in her breath. "Pardon me, ma'am."

"That's all right. You can take a message for me. You see, it's sort of embarrassing, but I left my new black nightgown—it was a Vanity Fair and cost me a lot of money—in our hotel room today, and I hope he found it. Could you just tell him to bring it tonight? I'd sure appreciate it. I don't mean to take up your time, but it cost me a lot of money."

She raised her voice to a wail. "Look, ma'am—"

"Avery. He'll know."

"I think you'll need to talk to him yourself. I have no business listening to such things, and I'm sure not going to relay any such thing to Mayor Price."

"You don't have to get worked up. I thought you'd understand, being a working person yourself. Those Vanity Fairs don't grow on trees."

She almost whispered in her distress, "Miss, my other line is ringing. Do you mind?"

Lying back in the bed, I let my mind poke around on the matter of reprisal, much as you press your tongue again and again around a toothache. The more I considered, the more I liked the idea of some public humiliation at which the Kraut in white socks could do no more than twitch his official face. As a plan took shape, so did its instrument. The time had come to call in my one outstanding debt—a handy thing to have owing when the ticks are out and the shopkeepers are getting rebellious.

"Congressman Vlasig's office. May we help you?"

"I'm calling from his home district to report a case of *crowpick*. This bird is after my eyes."

"Did you want a copy of our brochure on sheep diseases?" This one was on her toes, no honeyed fluster here. This was a seasoned pro used to dealing with loonies from the boonies.

"I want to talk to Willy. This is Avery Krause."

"I'm afraid he'll be tied up until after seven. He's in a caucus to work out a future bill to aid the independent rancher." She gave the information constituents needed to hear.

"This is his mistress. His *numero uno*, as we say in Texas."

"I'm afraid I'll have to break this connection." The telephone went dead in my ear.

When I had her back on the line I picked up where we left off. "I'm at a radio station in Prince Solms getting ready to go on the air to tell the voters how long it is, the tricks he does with it, and how many years we've been at it."

"We get calls such as yours twice a day, you know." She bluffed firmly.

"I'll hang up and you can call me back at radio KPAC. You might be interested to know that sitting here with me, a high six-figure check in his pocket, is a publisher who is taking notes this minute."

"If you'll leave us your number, Miss Krause."

"I'm not hanging up. *Crowpick* can be fatal."

"It might be that the congressman could return your call in a little while."

"Willy Vlasig sucks sheep."

She sighed. "Hold on. We'll see what we can do."

The thing about Willy was that he is the idol of the grandfathers. When he walked down the streets of Prince Solms the meager mercantile men in their suspenders and hats—their rolled-up shirt sleeves held with rubber bands, their beer bellies spilling over their belts—got in line to shake his fair hand. To the cotton-skirted wives with fat curls he was the son—not the big-footed, slow-thinking boys they had produced, but the son of their dreams. Sick of kitchen wars, they clung to Willy along with their memories of the old language, zinc plates, and wedding gowns. *Wir verheer lichen dich*, their eyes told him. We glorify you.

At last the line crackled. "Willy Vlasig here."

"This is Avery."

"Good God, I had no idea what back-home kook was on the line."

"A few choice chippies came to mind?"

"None who could drop *crowpick*. My secretary takes good notes."

"Then she related a few other phrases?"

"Enough to get the job done."

"I need you to repay a debt."

"This is a touch of blackmail for that tidy hatchet job you did on my opponent?"

"Right." This was a mutual fiction, of course. Willy would have won handily without my tape of the opponent protesting he was not a drunk. The sheepkeepers to the west knew full well he didn't know a nickel's worth about the ranching business; they voted for him out of their basic trust of rich men. Just as the grandfathers voted for him as the cream of the homeland. Other people had helped Willy as much as I; there was the TV station in coyote country which had spliced statements of Willy and his opponent so that it sounded as if it had been a taped debate, with the bad guy dodging the challenges. Willy was coming to my rescue not to return a favor, but because he liked to wield his power as often as possible; he had read that if you didn't exercise the muscle you got a case of atrophy.

"What did you have in mind?"

"His honor Sterling Price just threatened to get me fired from my job by spreading a little rumor about Otto and me."

"No sweat. I own controlling stock in the station."

"I didn't call for reassurance; I called for revenge."

"That generally takes us longer." He waited expectantly.

"I want us to hot-box him at Fiesta when he is surrounded by five hundred people and can't get away. I want Otto and me to go as dates, and you and Minna Raabe to come as the beautiful cosmopolitans, and us to reduce him to crawling across the floor."

"We could show at the opening ceremony when the king is crowned. No, wait—only fine old families and members of the Order can go inside the Alamo for that one; peons have to stand out front." He was silent on my nickel. "I'm thinking."

"Something lavish. I'm planning to go as Cinderella at the ball."

"I'm thinking. There's the Merienda-German out at the old mission. But no real Germans or Mexicans can come. Otto and I might be given the job of parking cars."

"Aren't there parties after the river parades?"

"Too small, too clubby. Your mayor couldn't get his foot in the door. I'm thinking." He left the phone for another spell. "All right, we've got it. The Queen's Garden Party. That's Friday week. Mabel tells me I can get away. It's a big outside bash at an old antebellum place with a reflecting pool. Big receiving line. Champagne. The Order pays everyone back so anyone who is anyone will be there. No peons, but all the loose money." He sounded delighted at the chance to do small-penny battle back home.

"Lovely. Can you get us all invitations?"

"I have them already, coming as I do from the landed gentry."

"Minna went on the video today spreading implications that she was your dearest friend."

"Can't beat that for PR. I'm glad you two got together; she can use some help."

"So can I."

"Mabel will let you know when to meet my plane."

"She may not want to speak to me again."

"Nothing bothers Mabel; that's why I have her."

"Thanks, Willy. Let me know when you're ready to run for the Senate."

"I'd be afraid not to."

I lay on my back and clapped my bare feet together, a monkey with a new trick. It was amazing how easy settling scores was when you got the hang of it, especially when you knew all the nuances of the medium already. Who better than one gifted at the uses and abuses of the Ear could manipulate that intrusion by voice, the telephone?

How disloyal I had been to our Theater of the Audible; what power would be lost if they could see that the thundering hoofs were after all only coconut shells.

ELEVEN

Cinderella at the Ball

Dressed in our party best, Minna and Otto and I waited an hour in the San Antonio airport, watching the planes skim under the clouds and coast down the runway.

Otto knew the city of San Antonio in which he had many relatives. He knew where everyone was welcome and where he was not. With his new solid confidence that he could play any part, he had cast himself in the only one in which he could be comfortable at the Queen's Garden Party: country music star. In an electric blue glistening tux, with his hair combed high and wide into an afro and his mustache pomaded into a twirl, he looked, arriving at the airport, as if the whole band should be following in his wake. Those who didn't know might think we were escorting Johnny Rodriguez, and even those who did might hesitate and look again.

Minna, less sure of herself, had come gowned in an elegant gray ankle-length skirt with a gray silk shirt cut almost to her waist, showing ropes of chains hiding discreet cleavage. She had added, for the locals who did not grasp understatement, the glitter of a gold chain belt and gold stilt sandals. Nervous that she might be overdressed, or even underdressed, it being a gala and all, she clung close to Otto, perceiving at once that he understood the reality of the caste system they were headed toward and that he would be friend enough to guide her through it.

I had come, of course, as the princess, in a yellow gown light as corn silk, its tight waist blossoming into a gossamer gathered skirt. My light hair was brushed free of frizzies and echoed the color of the dress. Then, remembering some fairy tale in which the princess danced all night in silver shoes in a silver wood, I had added platinum slippers.

Otto made conversation designed to put Minna at her ease. "Avery tells me you write for the papers in Washington?"

"I tell them that, too, Otto. Though if I don't get back up there soon they may advise me otherwise."

"Not much news back here."

"News is your business. Mine is little-known and seldom-remembered features."

"I give the grandfathers what they want to hear: that it will rain one day. That things could be worse. That what is happening is not going to hurt them in the pockets."

"If they believe all that, you must be good."

"They believe my voice when they hear it because it sounds like them." He laughed at his joke.

Exactly an hour late, the great glinting bird landed. "Watch this," I told them. "Here he comes."

As always, Willy was worth the wait. At the top of the ramp he paused: fair, blue-eyed Willy Vlasig, the Germans' lost youth. Then, chin up, he descended the steps, carrying two dozen long-stemmed yellow roses.

Inside the terminal, reporters clamored about him. "What brings you to town, Congressman?"

"Business and pleasure, gentlemen. I needed to see some women about some sheep." He indicated us to them.

"What about the bill to aid the independent rancher?"

"Later, gentlemen, later. We're on our way to sample the native beverage by the river front. If any of you would care to join us for a Lone Star?"

With newsmen Chuck and Bernie trailing us in their car, Willie explained the detour. "It seemed like a fine idea to drop off at Lupe's for a few *nachos*. Isn't he your kinfolk, Otto?"

"My uncle Lupe Ramirez who owns El Gato?"

"We might as well pay our respects."

Otto beamed. "He will be glad to see you, sir."

"Tonight I am Willy."

"To Lupe you are *Wee-lee*." Otto, master of the languages, performed. "To the Germans at home you are *Villy*."

"I can see you taught Avery here everything she knows."

"Some of it." Otto stroked his luxuriant mustache.

We stopped at a riverside cafe with iron tables and

striped awnings. Everyone knew Willy Vlasig; they had put him where he was today. The delighted proprietor, his brother, his brother's wife, and four waiters with napkins tucked in their belts rushed upon the distinguished guest.

"Wee-lee, long time no see."

"Can you pull up two tables, Lupe? For me and my friends." He indicated the trailing newsmen.

"Anything, Wee-lee. For you, everything is on the house. For your friends, also."

Perceiving that Lupe, in his excitement, had failed to recognize his brother's boy, Willy gave credit. "Otto insisted we come to your place."

"Otto, sure. Hey, boy. How's your papa? Look, Carlos, it's Jaime's boy."

"He's well. He looks the same."

At once we were presented with frosted mugs and chilled pitchers of the house's best dark beer. Warmed tortillas, snatched from some paying customer's table, were put before us.

Willy launched into an anecdote to charm the owners and feed the press—not to my surprise, he began with sheep. "So my aides told me—now you good people know that aides are those LBJ School fellows in Italian cotton shirts—'Think sheep, Willy.' Every day they rehearsed me. 'Who is man's best friend?' 'The sheep.' 'Who feeds the poor?' 'The sheep.' 'Who slept with your mother?' 'A sheep.'

"I studied the sheep-fact booklets—stiff stuff on enzootic abortion in scabby disease, written, so they claimed, in nontechnical language for the sheepman as wool grower, fat lamb producer, and stud breeder. I committed to memory pages on ram testicle abnormalities and Tasmanian braxy."

Chuck, the young acne-faced journalist, wrote feverishly, while Bernie, a veteran newsman with bags under his eyes, chain-smoked to show that he knew these tales were off-the-cuff fluff.

Lupe and his brother brought us a fresh pitcher while the waiters passed platters of peppery *nachos*.

"Then," the congressman continued, "I gerrymandered out to Ozona where the word was coyotes. Same drill. 'Why do you favor gun control?' 'We need to wipe out them coyotes.' 'How do you feel about poison pellets?' 'We need to get them coyotes.' 'What is the biggest threat to democracy in the world today?' 'The coyote.'" He allowed us time out for laughter.

At close range you could see, if you chose to, that the congressman was not all he seemed. You could see the dye job at the roots of his fair hair; spot the bright blue contact lenses; catch a suggestion of pancake on his even sunlamp tan. No matter, the effect was larger than life.

Resuming, he improvised. "My aides went into market research. 'We're going to sell you across the district in groups of twelve,' they said. 'A slight disciple overtone, don't you think, boys?' 'Do I walk on the Weser? Do we cater loaves and fishes?' 'Okay. Thirteen. You've definitely got thirteen-man charisma.' 'Unlucky number, fellows.' 'Goddamn it, Willy, then eleven. You have positively got eleven-man charisma.'

"I liked that. The elevens were easy multiplication on the chartered planes. I could doze counting elevens jumping the fence like sheep: twenty-two, thirty-three, forty-four . . . I figured that, in the end, I personally committed premeditated charisma on eighty-eight people a day."

The eleven of us around him applauded, all the more delighted as we suspected the story had been invented specifically for us.

As Willy rose, his performance finished, Lupe clapped him on the back. "Come again, Wee-lee. Anytime you come we are glad to see you. Bring your friends. Don't rush off. Otto, tell my brother, your papa, that he is going to outlive us all."

In the car Willy headed us toward the main performance. "Did you know," he asked, swerving through the honking cars, "the merino weighs two hundred seventy-five pounds when he drops his lamb teeth?"

"They loved you."

"When I run for the Senate, Otto can bring in San Antonio for me."

"I would be happy to do that, sir."

"What the hell do you say," Minna asked, "at the Queen's Garden Party?"

At the antebellum mansion, men waving flashlights guided us to the end of a long row of cars.

Other white-coated ushers guided us behind the peach-painted neo-Greek mansion, past a formality of rounded hedges and topiary trees, down a brick walkway outlined in pierced purple, orange, and red paper lanterns, to the splendor of a reflecting pool which floated flickering candles and fragrant gardenias. At the far end, Her Highness, flanked by a full entourage, received guests against a trellis

157

woven with a thousand fresh roses and as many twinkling lights. It was the stuff of fairy tales.

Helping ourselves to champagne, we got in line. As behind us four elderly dowagers reminisced about the old days when "we were in Coronation," and we all crept forward toward royalty, Willy filled us in on the players and their status. For example, the Order took only five married and fifteen unmarried men each year, all largely hereditary. Similarly, no more than four girls, the very cream of the cream of the fine old families, were considered for the coveted titles of princess and queen.

Several glasses later, at the glimmering, blooming trellis, the queen herself took our hands in her damp fingers. She was, in human form, the dog on the tapestry: the court greyhound, easily startled, held for viewing by a jeweled collar. Descended from a Vassar graduate known in legend as the first woman in Central Texas to drive her own car, she had paled that original spark to a dutiful passivity. "I'm Stuart Pascal Cleve," she introduced herself politely. "Welcome to the Queen's Garden Party." Stiff in opalescent seed pearls and glistening crystal baguettes, she passed us on to the president of the Order.

William Bennett IV appeared as a ruddy faced phantom of the opera, being clad in a black satin cloak over a black cutaway. If the queen's hand had been clammy, his was pink and hot. His porcine cheeks sagged from the weight of being the fourth Billy in his line, of being the plaster cast of an original model whose likeness had long ago been obscured.

"Good evening, Willy, I mean Congressman, we're glad to have you." He blushed eagerly at the honor. Perspiring lightly onto his heavy white collar, flinching and then recovering politely at the sight of Otto, he handed us on to the matron on his left, whom we learned was the president of the Battle of the Flowers.

At the far end of the receiving line, I caught sight of Sterling Price. Not prestigious enough to be a dignitary of Fiesta, but politician enough to attempt rank by association, he stood in a cluster of other such people, at the tag end of the official greeters. With him, wetting nervous lips, was a scrawny, hyper woman in a lime and aqua sequined gown. His wife, clearly. How fine. Somehow, in my rehearsal of the moment, I had forgotten her inevitable presence. Eagerly I cast about for Clarence and Alfred, but, alas, they were nowhere to be seen.

"—my friend, Minna Raabe from Washington," Willy was saying, moving us on down the line toward confrontation.

The actual moment surpassed my imagining of it. Sterling, looking up unexpectedly into the glowing visage of Willy Vlasig, stammered a merchant's greeting. "A privilege, a privilege—" Impressed by the silk-clad, dark-eyed beauty on the arm of the congressman, he grabbed her hand. "I don't believe we've met." Then, catching himself, he added quickly, "This is Mrs. Price, the wife."

Minna leaned over to give the mayor a cheek kiss. "Surely you're joking that you don't remember me? After the interview I did with you for the *Post*? Why, we talked four hours about your fat stock shows and your river parades and your prayer breakfasts; you were Washington's prize example of Texas provincialism."

The mayor, who knew he had never uttered a word to

this woman in his life, looked stricken—as his wife snatched at his arm to find out exactly what was going on here.

At that instant, casting his eyes about for help, Sterling caught sight of his onetime mistress with Otto Ramirez.

"You." He sagged visibly at what was becoming clear.

"Hello, Sterling." I said, nodding at lime and aqua. "You remember Otto; we were talking about him just the other day."

"Goot day, your honor." Otto gave it his best German voice. "Ve have missed you on our show."

"There's some mistake." Sterling tried to turn his back.

As he did, I leaned over toward his retreating ear to whisper, "Did you ever find that black nightie I left in our hotel room?"

"I'll call you later," he croaked hoarsely, taking the bony elbow of the mother of his sons and propelling her out of earshot.

All in all, it called for another round of champagne.

Poolside food tables, lit with luminaries and set with pots of orange and red flowers, offered cakes and coffee for those sobering, and spicy *buñuelos* and *anachuchos* for those of us still drinking.

As Willy informed us that each duchess' gown cost upward of seven thousand dollars, I waved at my old friend the wardrobe mistress. Fully co-ordinated with the party, she had on a one-shoulder festive designer gown of watered lavender taffeta, edged in waistline scallops of cerise and orange.

As I did, someone just past her bare shoulder waved back. His honor, the flustered mayor, come to drag me away from the crowd. "Can you come here for a minute," he beseeched.

Willy and Otto stepped on each side of me, instant bodyguards.

"At ease," I told them. "This is the scene I came for."

Sterling pulled me past the topiaries, behind the rounded hedges, into the garden of Diana and Artemis, amid urns of ferns nesting at the corners of low boxwood. "What the hell are you trying to do to me? That was the wife out there. I don't get it about that nightgown business; you know you never showed up at the hotel so how could you have left it there? And what's with showing up here with that Mexican from your station? This is the Queen's Garden Party. For God's sake, what's got into you?"

"They loved Otto. They thought he must be famous."

"You've been acting crazy ever since last week. Things were going fine, weren't they? You didn't complain. I thought you were satisfied." In a frenzy to patch things up he grabbed for me and pushed his tongue into my mouth.

For old times' sake I indulged in one final shopkeeper fantasy as the curtain fell:

Sterling had dropped his trousers about his ankles, where they bunched over the white socks, as, with his tight bare ass rising and falling, he mounted a shaggy tick-infested goat for the benefit of the assembled royalty. Murmuring huskily, "Easy, baby, easy," he clutched the tangled wool with both hands and rutted with his usual seriousness, some prurient dream behind his closed eyes. While, from above, robins rained gummy guano on his shoulders . . .

Wrenching myself away from him, I said, "It doesn't pay

to threaten the working class. You failed to assess all the possible results."

"I didn't mean all that. You got me all upset when you didn't show up."

"You better get out of this garden and tend to Mrs. Price. She looked as if her eye could find your needle in any haystack."

"I told her I had gone to get some coffee."

"Take care, Sterling. Send me pictures of the boys at Christmas."

"I just don't get it." Puffing, angry, he tucked his shirt back into his black trousers and ran past the stone lovers.

Our chores done, we drove downtown to La Villita, a river-front cluster of artisans' shops, sidewalk sweets, beer, and booths where children and drunks could swing poles at gaudy *piñatas*—breaking the decorated clay animals open to shake loose colored candies inside. Giddy with the success of my venture, I handed my dozen yellow roses to a crippled old lady in a shawl and hiked up my skirt to mingle with the fifty thousand others eating cotton candy, snow cones, *pan dulce*, and longneck beer.

Caught up in the mood, Willy raised his voice in a clear bell-like tone to sing the German national anthem. To which no one paid attention, as it mingled with the general din.

"I can yodel," Otto offered. And did so in fine style.

"All we need," Minna said, "is a sheep to lead around by the collar and we'd win best of show."

"Did you know the Rambouillet came to this country

the same year as the Germans? And they have never inter-married."

"Make him cease, desist." Minna took Otto's arm. "Take me to get something to eat. Something hot and greasy before I'm too drunk to stand up."

"Let's sit," I told Willy, pulling him to a table out on the sidewalk. "Cinderella needs to get out of these slippers."

"Whenever I think I need to mix with the voters, I should come down for this; half of my electorate must be here in the village."

"I love all this. The blobs and sticks and platters of food. And everybody in costume, all making movies. It's a real ball; much classier than the Queen's Garden Party."

Willy hooked us each a beer from a tired waitress, slipping a five-dollar bill into her hand. Drinking from the sweating bottles, we had ringside seats for the milling mob. The woman in the shawl to whom I had given my roses, no longer crippled, hawked them in the crowd. "Get your Yellow Rose of Texas here, only one dollar."

"Have you run into a writer named Bill Albrech?" Willy asked. "Old German family, his grandfather a cousin of mine or some such. Used to work for the San Antonio *Light*. Used to say they only let him cover the outer core of the inner city. He did a fine job for me during the campaign; a master at the rewrite of the sheep tale. Somebody told me he just dropped out. Went to the Dobie Ranch to get it together, or however they say it."

I think I felt the blow before I heard it. Behind my eyes swam the image of rundown, brown, scuffed shoes. "He's living with his grandfather," I reported.

"No kidding? You never can tell, can you? Well, if you see him, remind him there's always a job waiting."

It had been a mistake to drink beer on top of champagne on top of beer. "Some of my best friends are Germans," I told our congressman.

"Around here that's safe enough." He drained his glass. "Or was that meant as a kind gesture to present company? I think my reflexes are getting slow."

"So are mine."

"Hey." Unsteadily, Willy got to his feet and pointed in the general direction of the mob. "Isn't that Minna over there?"

Sure enough, it was. To the left of the swirling multitudes a dozen eighteen-year-olds with long hair, satin blouses, and pirate pants with knives tucked in their sashes ringed the frightened easterner in gray silk. "Wouldja look at this," one of them, drunk, shouted, pointing to our friend in the middle of the circle. "Wouldja look at this." He had on one earring, a shirt open to the waist, and a slash of red painted on his lips. "Wouldja look at this, everybody? This lady has on matching shoes and belt. Did you ever think you'd see that again? I'm so fucking tired of hippies, little lady; I'm so fucking tired of all this ethnic dress. You've got class, lady, with them matching shoes and belt. Hey, fellas, let's sing a song for the little lady in her golden belt. Come on, ring around the rosy . . ."

As Willy headed to the rescue, Otto reached out a hand to stop him. "Don't get excited, sir. Queen Esther will take care of it."

Sure enough, from the crowd Jane Brown, in her black crepe and garnet brooch, broke through the circle of fugitives from Peter Pan. "You boys should be ashamed of yourselves, making a spectacle of her in a public place. Didn't your mothers teach you any manners? With one strong arm she pulled Minna free. "Get along, now. Get on along."

She turned to the young woman, lines of worry on her face. "Did they harm you?"

"Those guys were weird. Next time I come down to the sticks I'm not bringing anything but bluejeans and boots."

"A fine disguise," I told her, having learned it was true.

Willy confiscated two chairs from a nearby table. "Mrs. Brown, won't you join us?"

"Hello, William. How have you been?"

"Not up to your standards, I'm afraid."

"I'm so proud of you up there."

"I'm proud of you down here." Willy became a student again before her.

"Child." She turned to Minna. "I think you must ask for these scenes."

"It's her fate," Otto explained.

"Down here I forget I have to watch out for cars." Minna shuddered. "I need a keeper."

"By that I would hope you do not mean a man." With that Jane Brown rejoined three bulky women who had waited silently on the sidewalk for her.

"Shall we have another round or call it a night?" Willy put a protective arm around Minna's gray shoulder, rallying from the alcohol to the rescue.

"Once over lightly while I catch my breath and take off this damn belt."

Otto moved in to protect her other flank, showing by his loyalty his defense of her against the straggly pirates.

I stared out at the costumed mob. You never learned. Each time you shut your eyes, convinced the frog you kissed would turn. If not this one, then the next one. Green, bloated bastards all of them puckering up those slimy lips in fraud. They never meant to change; they just put that rip in their psyche, that hair on their belly, that scuff on their shoes to lure you to the pond. They never mean to turn.

Still another time I had fallen for someone who did not exist. When Henry first came into my class in a top hat with a white scarf that reached the floor, a magician, I said why not and went immediately to bed. Last week I said why not, ignite your bloody eggs in the fire and hump me on the rocks. None of us are German, are we, Billy Wayne, I said. How long since you've been back here to Texas? . . .

Otto handed me the final Lone Star of the night. Taking my silence for concern, he offered solace. "Queen Esther took care of it for her," he said.

I considered my beer. "It seems the writer moved even slower than we thought."

TWELVE

Papa Placed Among the Shells

The uncle could hold out no longer; face to the wall, they said, he died. Grandfather sank into grief. His moist thick lips, his bulbous nose, his protruding eyes swelled in vain to encompass emotions too large for his conceiving. To lose his last brother amid the shrieks of Olga Dolle that the only son must that same day be set among the clabber-eating Swedes, be plucked from the ground where God intended him to lie, was too vast a blow.

As Mama and I piled into the car to meet Otto and the old gravediggers, Grandfather set out with his dog Rufus across the field. *Sohn der Familie Krause* existed for him no longer. Beside me, chest rising and falling, Mama was a swelling apparition in floating white dimity above white hose and spiked white shoes. "It isn't needed to wear black any more," she informed me.

"This is navy." In some crazed confusion, I had succumbed to the old rhyme of something old (Papa), something new (his reappearance), something borrowed (the Swedish plot), something blue (me). In an attempt to lend some sketchy stability to the event, I had worn the same bulky skirt and jacket that attended his burial the first time.

Otto, in his black sexton's suit, had brushed his mustache into a downcast mien and combed his hair flat and parted it in the middle. This Monday morning at the end of April neither of us bore much resemblance to our festive, Fiesta selves.

A dozen shell-encrusted graves lay within the Dolles' lacy fence. The oldest weathered ones on the left marked Jaar and Sophie; the newest on the right commemorated Carl and Bertha. Past them, Papa's space gaped across the back, end to end with four other vacant spots, one of which would be Mama's.

While she instructed the silent old men, I made small graveside talk with Otto. "Whatever happened to pine boxes?"

"They caved in. You could tell who had been buried in a box because his plot sank below the ground."

"Making his family look cheap."

"We now require a metal casket."

"Handier the second time around, I can see."

"Your mama is determined."

"She wanted him out before they turned the first spade on Uncle. No one must be allowed to rest in peace."

Mama tugged at my arm. "Look over there. What are those nigras doing here?"

Otto and I turned to see Jane Brown, in a black faille suit, with a tall young man, standing some distance from her car.

"Those are friends of mine, Mama."

Otto nodded. "You go. I will look after things here."

"You can't leave me," Mama whispered frantically, teetering on her tiny toes away from Otto, "with the Mexican."

"I'm leaving you in the hands of God, Mama."

I opened the delicate Dolle gate, and then the filigreed Swedish one, touched that these visitors had come.

"Good afternoon, Avery. Otto told me your father was to be buried."

"This is an encore."

"So he said. All the more painful, no doubt. I thought it fitting, as we are to be associated on your radio show, that we pay our respects. Have you met my Theodore?"

Dark as bittersweet chocolate, her son had on a glistening white shirt and a white tennis sweatband. A full foot above me, he bent down to make eye contact. "Hi."

"You're the basketball coach?"

"At least you didn't say, 'How's the air up there?'"

"I had to bite my tongue."

"How come the uncles are digging a place for your old man again? This gonna be an annual event?"

"I'm afraid to ask."

Jane interrupted us. "I felt I should put in an appearance, whether I was welcome or not." Resolutely, she indicated Mama's distraught, staring face. "It seemed a courtesy."

"I'm glad you did. Otto and I were getting a little spacy."

Theodore bent down. "You know what you're getting into, putting my mom on your show?"

"I may, but the grandfathers don't."

"I am anticipating my role," Jane let us know firmly. "You said to inform you when I was ready to begin, and I believe I have prepared my part. How would Monday morning suit you?"

"That would be grand." I was caught off guard at the suddenness of it. How pleased Otto would be to have arranged this coup for us. Was I supposed to volunteer the club news for her to read? We had not talked money, which was awkward, as I had also not mentioned this new persona to the station managers.

"I will come fully prepared. You may rely on that."

"I'm very pleased."

Her missions accomplished, Jane touched her son's arm in a gesture of dismissal. To me she added, "Don't take her grievances on yourself, child. Nothing is to be gained by that. It only loses you energy from your own purposes."

"Yes, ma'am."

"Take care, hear?" Theodore waved good-by.

"Thank you for coming," I told them both.

Back at the site, Mama reproached me for desertion. "It's not natural for you to be talking to those people."

"They are friends."

"This is your papa's funeral."

"I know, Mama. Here I am."

As the hole grew deeper and she rocked back and forth, I gave her bulk a gentle squeeze. How could you ever tell what was you within such a mound of flesh? It must be that for her the more of her there was the safer it felt. Whereas Minna felt less herself with each obscuring pound.

"Gustav would not come," she reminded me.

"He is mourning his brother, Mama." And, of course, no less, his son.

"He thinks his Germans a cut above us. Ever since I married he tells Gus we were nothing. What does he know? We were not immigrants. Our Svante Palm was a learned man; he brought to this country ten thousand books. We did not cling to the old languages. We did not put our heads in the sand. We have standards. They teach us there is no need to bow and scrape before gentlemen." High on Mama's cheeks sprang the telltale flash of color.

She kneaded her hands into a doughy ball. "They wanted a German son from me. 'Give us a grandson, Dolly,' he would tell me. 'You must give your Gus a son, Olga,' Mother Krause would say. For them, I would not. For myself I made a girl. When I finally got you out—such a bloody little thing to hurt me so like that—I sat up to see if it was morning yet. That was my good luck. Out the window was that big red grocery sign, it was before your time to remember it, of AVERY'S MARKET. That was a name which counted for something. It was the name of one who owned something."

The creases in her chins were unmoving as the past came tumbling from her lips. "'What a sweet babe,' they said to me after. "'We will name her Maria Magdelena,' they said, making winks over my head, claiming my newborn. I who all night had held my stomach while the baby tore me to pieces. I said to myself then, if I lived, my girl was going to belong to me; for the Germans I would not make another hired girl. 'Her name is Avery,' I told them. 'That isn't in the family,' they said to me.' 'It is now,' I told them."

She sucked in her breath. "I evened the score for the way they treated me. I took the language from their church. By myself I got the Swedes behind me and Gus to come along. By our two votes I won. Now I have taken their Gus from them. Let everyone see where he belongs. My ways are not their ways. I don't mind saying who is to blame. God is not a German no matter what they tell you."

With this last outburst Mama's tiny arches gave way. Her hand-span ankles turned under the weight of the last retribution. She begged, "Help me to sit down."

She wound down. "Gustav still thinks himself the master but he no longer has me to do for him." Dabbing at her damp cheeks and streaming eyes, she jabbed out her final words. "Mother Krause is no longer there to light the fire to make his soup. His Dolly will be no longer there to make his dumplings. I have a place to move. I have the money." With pride, she patted the secret pouch beneath the dimity.

"I have rented a room behind the police station to the right of the lumberyard. Do you know the little house, Avery? It has a back porch for myself. There is a window box. I have the money."

"Do you have a nice kitchen?" The memory of her in the brick-faced house away from the coal mines came back to me clearly as today—her humming her tunes, baking her crisp and lacy sweets, unfolding her tiny paper flowers.

She blinked her watery blue eyes. "A hot plate is enough for one."

"Does Grandfather know you're leaving?"

"If he wishes to know it he can ask my people. They will tell him."

I remembered, also, Papa in that brand-new house, marking debits and credits in ledgers which kept account of cash transactions and covenants extracted; Mama's contentment unacceptable to a son raised to the wringing of necks, clothes, and sighs. His closed ways making a wall around her joy; repeating Grandmother, in her shimmy, venting her anger at the willful waywardness of the son's wife.

᠈ Yesterday feinted at every turn, parried your versions of old times, pierced you with new ones. At playing hoaxes on the Eye and Ear the past emerged the master; behind the gossamer curtain it held up fingers for rabbit ears and locked thumbs and flew its hands for birds. Deceiving you, it made illusion behind the screen of recollection.

Mama had kept herself a Swede on purpose, had excluded herself from the Germans to survive. Had also, at the start, marked me and set me apart so they could not claim me. Much as, in fairy tales, the princess is blessed with a special mole or strawberry mark, which, in the end, saves her from the wicked king.

Long overdue, I perceived the puffed and blimpy overlay on that young girl, who had smiled out from the photograph at happy ever after, as bulk against the German conquerors. Saw that Mama had incorporated vast amounts of self in order to remain an immigrant in their oppressive midst. Saw that she had made pale hair, thin chest, flaring legs like mine the mark of those who stood outside the fold.

"Hey, Mama." I patted her gross and dimpled knees. Proud to be one Swede comforting another.

At my touch she sniffed audibly, content to allow the tears to gush down her white cheeks and splash on her soft sprigged bosom. "The last time they did not let me mourn my Gus. Before, they stuffed my mouth with a handkerchief." Remembering, she began to wail, as was her due.

"The grave is ready, ma'am." Gingerly, Otto intruded his suitably solemn countenance.

The old blacks, leaning on their hoes and wiping their brows, awaited a signal from the fat lady who had hired them.

Mama jabbed me with an elbow. "Get him to help."

With Otto unfurling, Mama spread a Swedish flag, golden cross on bright blue field, upon the casket. Otto guided the old men and the box through the lowering. When the casket struck bottom we all shook from the force of it. As the diggers began to toss dirt in upon the box she tore from the sod a piece of emerald German ivy and flung it into the hole; ripping out strands of her hair, she tossed them in as well. Bending until her marbled legs touched the ground, she flung in a handful of dry dust. "Now you see how we get back at those who think water is thicker than blood."

Carefully the men lay the sodded ivy on top of the mound—a deep green plot among the white sea shells.

Her head bouncing up and down in satisfaction over this final blow—the theft of the son from the grandfathers—

reminded me, in its exultation and its force, of me lying on my bed, naked, clapping my feet together at the first sweet taste of revenge against the mayor.

Why had I not seen that everything I learned was at my mama's dimpled knee?

Attempting to emulate Grandmother Magdelena, I had again and again come up against the fact that the unspoken protest, the covert and passive way of banged doors, pursed lips, and winding sheets was not the style for one who dealt in the ear-stabbing intrusion of telling it out loud. Grandmother's silent ways served, after all, only to preserve the status quo of her control over sweat-soaked BVDs and plucked and headless hens.

Olga, on the other hand, her corkscrew curls bobbing and her little heels teetering, had boldly tilted at the very totems of the Germans—their church and their tongue and their heirs—and felled them all.

Her job finished, Mama settled on the grave, much as the white cat guarded Ybarra's pink niche among the clump of plastic lilies. "You're as good as any of them, Mama. Don't you forget it."

Then, letting her be, I ambled off into the sunshine.

THIRTEEN

Jane Brown Presents Herself

Otto and I were nervous as parents at a child's piano recital. We had invited Minna, due back at her paper the
next day, to be with us for moral support. After all, she
had dealt with the media in the Big Banana, as Willy calls
Washington; she knew how to reach an audience. She
would understand our jitters at becoming Avery, Otto,
and Aunt Jane.

The station managers had been prepared, although they
failed to see the use of two women on this four-hour
stretch of time, and, certainly, were not let in on why it
was such a joke to have a retired, educated black woman
tell about the pancake suppers. But then, I kept their adver-

tisers happy and selling, and Jane had accepted a token fee in return for becoming part of our show.

What I expected, what we all expected, was not what entered the studio door on the stroke of eight o'clock. Our guest for the day was to be, naturally, our new team member. My questions, thought out in advance, intended to focus on her seven national charities and play down such matters as her years teaching in the local schools. The more they imagined her to look as she sounded, a cultured lady bountiful, the better.

Jane Brown arrived, however, unmistakably as Queen Esther of the Missionary Baptist Church. She wore a long flowing crimson brocade robe which dragged the floor, and, on her marcelled, waved hair, she had placed a sort of tinseled coronet. In her hand she carried a fluted paper fan whose gentle watercolors depicted Jesus at the Mount of Olives. Straining, you could hear a choir behind her singing "Almost Persuaded"; squinting, you could see the Total Immersion of a dozen true believers.

Minna and Otto were appalled. Otto took me aside as he saw her come through the door. "She has missed the point. I do not see how. I told her it was the way that I sounded to the Germans, the same as them. I told her she could sound the same as a society lady from the East." He mopped his brow, distressed to his solid center by this mistake. Having figured out the way to make jokes, he could not comprehend that someone as respected as she would not get the point as well.

Minna sank down into the visitor's chair until she sat on the middle of her spine. In bluejeans, her new protective costume, she suffered the mental equivalent of hives. Whis-

177

pering hoarsely, "For God's sake, it was a Come As You Are Party and she didn't read her invitation."

"Good morning, Avery, Minna, Otto. It's a pleasure to be here beginning a new era in the lives of all of us."

I greeted her and tried to make her feel welcome in the stunned silence, not quite certain how to remark on her fantastic ensemble. I was delighted by it; and by the implications of her wearing it. Obviously this was to be the start of much tilting at windmills. I hoped both *Die Ältern* and *Los Protectores*, those alliances of old men, had cupped their ears in our direction. "I had thought we would call you Aunt Jane. I see that you have cast yourself in another parts. Is it to be Queen Esther?"

"Certainly, child. Wasn't that your understanding of our agreement from the start?"

"That's what Otto called you—" My sidekick flinched. "May I get you a cup of coffee?"

"You see that I have brought you a gift, Avery, on the occasion of the start of what I trust will be a long association. As I do not intend to drink your instant coffee, I have purchased for you an electric percolator."

Folding the fan with one hand, she offered me the bulky gift-wrapped pink package with the other.

"Thank you. That's very kind. We needed it." I took the present, remembering another that had arrived as we did. "Willy Vlasig sent a dozen yellow roses for your opening on the show."

"That boy is too extravagant." But clearly she was touched by her old student's gesture. These acknowledgments made, she looked about at all of us. "Well, then, shall we commence? Where do you wish me to sit?"

Warming our audience up, Otto reported a faint possibility of rain, and then I played Willie Nelson rendering "Amazing Grace," that being the nearest to gospel I could lay my hands on.

"Why don't I introduce you next," I told her, "here in the booth, and then you can tell them whatever you want to about what you're going to do. Then, at the last, we'll let you present a few women's items, as a preview of how you'll do it from now on."

On the other side of the pane of glass Minna lit a cigarette. Blowing a smoke ring, she wiped her palms on her jeans and sent me a grim look, as if to remind me it was my head on the block and not hers.

Then we proclaimed the good news over the air: "Good morning, fans, this is Avery Krause on KPAC, Keep Peace. The station which brings you morning now brings you tidings of great news, which is that from this day forth Queen Esther Brown of the Missionary Baptist Church will bring us those choice items of female industry, arts, and crafts to which many of you apply your talents and in which all of you take an interest. As the newest member of our radio team, she will be our special guest this morning, so that you can make friends with her at the start. Now, Queen Esther, tell us how it is that you decided to take time from your national philanthropies and lifelong labor for black education to join our show?"

"God took me by the hand and led me to the appointed place." Her cultured voice now took on the high mesmerizing pitch of the evangelist. "Tell them the News, Esther, He said to me. Give them the Word."

Minna got up and left the studio. Otto's solid face looked

as if he had just witnessed his mother's impact with the wall of water.

"Your presence here is our gain. Tell me, Queen Esther, how do you see yourself interpreting those things that fill the days of our local women?" With full confidence I fed her the cues that would allow her to play out her audacious part.

"The Lord has instructed them to be about His business. I intend to report each warp and woof in the loom of their stewardship."

"You mentioned that you were raised right here in Prince Solms?"

"That is true, Avery. As we established when we met, your grandmother and I played together as little girls on Corn Hill. No one knows the entire fabric of this town better than I, which will equip me to serve as your new club and civic reporter."

"You mentioned a strong feeling that one owed one's own community first allegience. I understand you encouraged your son also not to leave here but to put his athletic talents to use in the place where he got his start." It seemed fair enough to give a plug to the basketball star.

"That is correct. My Theodore coaches for Consolidated High during the week and for the Lord on the Sabbath, both right here among his own people." Her tone admonished the German listener that the latter applied to him.

With that we gave the air back to music in order to provide our listeners time to flood the station with their calls. Which they did:

"I think you're just marvelous, I mean, that's so liberal

of you and all." The first caller shouted shrilly in my ear, acknowledging that the race and background of our new cohort had been fully and unmistakably revealed.

"—the last time I'm listening to your show, I can tell you that, little lady."

"You folks don't know your ass from your elbow out there, putting that kind of business on the air, like we got time to listen to them—"

"I'm calling, miss, from down here at the bank, to say that we all have a lot of respect for your Mrs. Brown, she's an outstanding lady no matter what—"

The calls broke about fifty-fifty, during which time Jane sat bold and pleased in her ruby robe and silver crown, facing the space vacated by Minna.

I wanted everyone to see her, to relish her performance, to delight in her dazzling pageantry. I wanted to be Camera Number Two zooming in on her until that resolute head beneath its glittering crown, or those wrinkled, clasped hands, unmoving on the brocade lap, consumed the viewer's retina. Longing for sight, I again conceded an all-too-apparent fact: the Eye is less inclined to lie. It might be that in good time I would have to wrest from Terry Lynn Taylor, not her station manager's bed, or her green beads, but her midday spotlight. What could be finer across your kitchen table than a view of things as they truly are, brought to you by Avery, Otto, and Queen Esther?

After a sensual Robert Flack song, and after I had reintroduced our new performer for those who tuned in late, Jane got to speak for herself. Which she had intended all along.

"For those of you whose grandmothers stitched on home looms scraps and squares from cherished garments, the Ladies' Aid Society of the Evangelical and Reform Church has arranged a quilting bee and sale this Saturday at the Sophie Fairgrounds. A prize of a one-hundred-year-old quilt depicting the Lone Star will be raffled by the lemonade stand at four in the afternoon. Tickets may be purchased . . ."

Today Queen Esther presented only benign and ecumenical news, her voice and her name being performance enough for this opening shot. When she had told them all good morning, we let Otto labor through the local and national news, both steaming up now in the month of May, and went in search of Minna.

Who leaned against the fence where I had received the red bandana from the closet-German writer.

Minna had her back to us, staring off at nothing. Without turning, she started in. "I couldn't help it. I couldn't listen to you. I can't understand any of it, why anyone would stick herself out like that for ridicule when I spend my whole life avoiding it."

"That's a waste of energy, then," Jane reprimanded. "I thought it high time the patriarchs in this town had to deal with the existence of a woman they did not control, which in this day and time still means a Negro, as they have their own females in a state of bondage. I thought it high time to make them sit up and listen."

"You can get into enough trouble in this world simply standing still without asking for it, Mrs. Brown. Obviously it's time I got back to the capital where I know exactly what's happening. At least the monogrammed towels and engraved stationery are safe. There are no nasty surprises about what's what: even if it has to mean he isn't calling and he isn't coming by. I can take anything but being out there in the middle of the street with all the fingers pointing."

"You're a quitter, child."

"You've got it wrong, Mrs. Brown. I was never even a starter in the races you're talking about. I'm not quitting; I'm just not entering." Minna turned around at that, her face streaked and smudged, but tight and closed. "What the hell is this going to do to you, Avery? You had a piece of cake going with your little show."

"I can always go back to teaching kids how to pretend they're rabbits turning into hats."

"I don't get it, the way you two can be so casual about it. You, especially, Mrs. Brown, when all you had to do was be that school principal with the glasses down on her nose and that goddamn flapping black cape, and give them your chocolate cake recipe."

"It doesn't do to stand still. I did what I believed would achieve the most in the long run. You can't rest on your past laurels."

"You actually want to make trouble." Minna almost shouted this at the old woman.

"They've said that about us for years, dear." Jane turned to me. "I hope I have your co-operation in this."

"I love Queen Esther. I think she'll be the best part ever played on this meager miserly German stage."

"Then if you're behind me, we shall have to handle as best we can the unease of your friends and your audience."

"Otto will be all right." I smiled, thinking of that faithful man, perplexed, troubled, reading his clips on outbreaks abroad and drought at hand, his trusting face furrowed by what he considered to be her failure to get the point.

"What can we do for this talented woman who intends to remain dependent on an obviously unsuitable affair?" Jane kept her eyes on Minna as she asked me.

"Oh, leave me alone, can't you? Your kind, who achieve yourselves to death, always put more on the rest of us than we can handle. You can't believe I wouldn't want to be a concert pianist even if I could. I don't even want to be the greatest living newswoman in the world, how do you like that? All I want is not to be ringed by a gang of crummy pirates."

"You're correct, that causes me distress." Jane reached out a firm hand to pat the brittle shoulder which drew back from her touch.

After our replacement arrived Jane invited us all to the Alpen Haus for potato pancakes, and, once there, proceeded to probe Otto about the women in his family tree; a long interrogation which included consolation about his mother, scolding for his fear of marrying, and a lengthy, gratuitous lecture against the Catholic stand on birth control.

It had not turned out as either he or I had expected that day we drove to Memorial Gardens to see what a place with no fences was like. Then—before the appearance of our friend with the cut-glass eyes or the woman who had now taken firm control of us all—it had seemed easy enough to add another audio-pun to our show.

Instead, I had learned a lot about those of us who pass

for others. Those of us who try, as Minna said, to be more like everyone else than everyone else. Here, taking her leave of us in a public place, an elderly woman in a flowing red robe provided an example for us all. Like Olga Dolle stuffing her Swedish ways down the throats of the grandfathers, Jane Brown's electing to go forth as Queen Esther demonstrated that winners were the ones not afraid to say they were others and act upon it.

Otto passing as German, Gruene passing as Czech, Minna passing as invisible, and Avery passing as a third-rate princess waiting in the wings of her garage tower could all take lessons.

Our hostess rose, signifying that we were adjourned.

"See you in the morning, Jane." I decided it was more than time to use this woman's given name.

"I shall count on that. God willing and the creek don't rise." She gave us the old, rote Texas parting.

Otto got up, too. "It sure took me by surprise, Queen Esther, you coming in like that."

"The rest of them, too, I trust."

FOURTEEN

A Prince of a Fellow

The day I went to confront the writer, KPAC, the station which brings you morning, almost put us all back to bed.

Worn out from an afternoon of spading around in vain for an interviewee, I had fallen into the old trap of having on the air, at the last minute, someone who had seemed outrageously funny in print. The media don't mix. Combing the weekly paper for a local willing to show on short notice, I had spotted a grand headline: SECOND ANNUAL SOPHIE COUNTY FAIR BEECHNUT CHEWING TOBACCO SPITTING CONTEST. The rules for the contest stated that there would be two main events: one testing accuracy, the other determining distance. Only true spit would count; no foreign matter would be allowed. Amazing. Having done a May

Fête queen and a Lion's Club vice-president already that week, this seemed the jolliest opportunity ever.

It wasn't. "Brushy" Koehler, the judge, not one to be caught with his pants down with all his neighbors listening, answered every question with the same two facts: "Yup, there'll be jest two events, the one for accuracy, don't you know, and the one for distance. . . ."

I padded him with songs and added my own patter about the return of the mud daubers to Luckenbach and the annual Terilingua chili cookoff, proving how our fine Texas events every year made nationwide news. No matter. His response remained the same: "Yup, jest your true spit will be allowed."

Despite my insistence that he could give no commercial, Brushy concluded by telling all our listeners, if there were any still tuned in, that "Beechnut's the tobacco I chew."

"You should have got him to tell you about tobacco stains on dentures," Otto said, when we had seen our guest out the door.

"Where were you when I needed you?"

Then, adding delay to recalcitrance, our replacement on the show was late. Waiting, we played a couple of songs from Jerry Jeff Walker's "Viva Terilingua" and made talk about the upcoming hot, dry season. At last Jimbo the deejay stumbled in, pleading a hard night, by which he meant drugs and not sex. Deep into his role as early freak, in leather jacket, stringy hair, and straggling beard, he cast himself in a movie ten years behind the times. Actually a radio-television-film major at the university, he conveyed to his fans that he went through life with fear and loathing, ate acid in the afternoon, and grooved on his daily three-hour slot of nonstop concrete rock.

Seeing us edgy, he flung down his jacket and grabbed up his stack of platters. "Hey, man, how's it going?"

He snapped his fingers and unbuttoned his black shirt another notch. "Hey, chick, why the long face?"

Fond of reruns, I was going to be sorry when Jimbo was replaced by someone spouting CB jargon.

From the university office which administered the Dobie Ranch, I got directions on how to get there. "You go fourteen miles southwest of town toward the historic hill country."

A cultured voice apparently read directions.

"Do I take the Sophienburg road?"

"I'm sure, I don't . . . let me see. Here: 'It is on swift-running, scenic, serpentine Barton Creek.' "

"Thank you very much."

"Would you like the telephone number? We are permitted to give that out."

"No, no phone number. The name of a farm-to-market road?"

" 'Its mascot, the symbol for the ranch, that curious and attractive roadrunner, bears the Mexican nickname of *paisano*.' "

"Thanks a lot. Really."

I set out to follow the back roads along Barton Creek until I found Billy Wayne, driving spring-driven needles into his rented mattress.

I came in his uniform, tan jeans and white shirt, to say

that there were other ways to tell the players besides by their costumes.

I followed weathered signs of a long-tailed roadrunner over cattle guards and through creaking gates. Finally, crossing the creek itself, on a low-water bridge, I pulled up into a wide field. Before me, set back under live oaks, was a farmhouse with tin German roof, stone chimney, and wide gallery porch. Hanging from the largest tree was an old wagon wheel, an inner tube, and a dinner bell. Behind the house stood the remains of horse stalls and milking shed, and, past that, far off, sheer limestone cliffs above the far curve of the creek. Goats dotted the distant cliffs; a salt lick for deer lay at the fence line.

Stepping onto the low porch, I took a deep breath and called out loudly. "Bill? Are you there?"

There was no answer, no bounding dog; I shoved open the screen.

There he sat, in a brown pullover and dark brown corduroy pants—old clothes that had once beat the pavement. He worked a manual typewriter, on a low table between his knees. His face was closed.

"I came to check the weather," I told him. "You're looking cloudy."

He stood up. "I wish you hadn't."

"As long as I did—?"

"Look around. I'll heat some coffee." He turned from me then and headed toward the shedlike kitchen to the back. His eyes had gone quite dark; his mouth had set in a line.

Invited to do so, I looked around. Invading his privacy in all directions.

Over the fieldstone hearth, suicide notes on half sheets of newsprint were tacked one above the other:
From John Berryman:

> I feel a final chill. This is cold sweat
> that will not leave me now. Maybe it's time
> to throw in my own hand.

> I don't think I will sing
> Anymore just now;
> or ever. I must start
> to sit with a blind brow
> above an empty heart.

Then, an Anne Sexton:

> . . . I am rowing, I am rowing,
> though the wind pushes me back
> And I know that that island will not be perfect,
> it will have the flaws of life,
> the absurdities of the dinner table,
> but there will be a door
> and I will open it
> and I will get rid of the rat inside me . . .

Two, pinned together, from e. e. cummings, very yellowed:

> In the middle of a room
> stands a suicide
> sniffing a Paper rose
> smiling to a self. . . .

the mind is its own beautiful prisoner.
Mine looked long at the sticky moon
opening in dusk her new wings
then decently hanged himself, one afternoon.

"Cheery," I commented, as he handed me a mug of strong, reheated coffee.

"Not for public consumption."

"These belong to you, or are they the grandfather's?"

He stood near the mantel also, as if to sit would encourage me to stay. "Hard to say." He looked past me. "Why did you come out here?"

"Our congressman told me some story about a San Antonio newsman, an ace reporter on sheep tales, from a fine old German family. Just a local boy who made good right beneath our noses."

He was silent. Then, "Willy dyes his hair and stuffs his jockey strap."

"No matter. At least his lies are visible to the eye." I waved a disbelieving hand at the scraps above the hearth, which seemed to me one more pose, one more imitation of writer's angst. "Do you have it off while reading these?"

"If I do, at least it's efficient, and doesn't interfere with my book."

"As opposed to visitors?"

"As opposed to visitors." He wore no belt. His baggy trousers had seen better days. Their seat was frayed. The old clothes, which should have been revealing, as the scuffed shoes had been, were not. He seemed a stranger. Even the brown hair brushed straight back from his wide forehead altered him. He looked older. As if he had been around. As if he had in fact come from the outer core of the inner city.

Moving from the mantel, seeing that I looked about with curiosity, he gave me a reluctant, cursory tour of the old farmhouse with its slanted plank floors and beamed ceilings. The door to his bedroom stayed closed; his pile of papers uncommented upon. "That's Dobie's handmade desk over there." He finished back by the couch. "The walls are three feet thick in some places. The original house ended there, at the entrance to the kitchen."

"You always do your research."

"Don't bait me."

Angry that he had deceived me, I was nonetheless aware what my intrusion cost him. There was no doubt I was in his room. Looking about for its other occupant, I asked, "Where is the dog?"

"Working. In the field."

"Let's go find her."

"Him. Ralph."

"That's what dogs say when they bark. Ralph, ralph."

Seizing on the chance to get me out of there, he pushed open the door and indicated the neutral ranchland.

In the muggy heat, we walked in silence, through high meadow grass under distant circling birds, taking our chances with snakes and chiggers and ticks, wading in forage and flowers.

"He usually goes down to the creek." Bill Albrech made bare conversation, as if to the uninvited acquaintance who appears at the wrong time when you are expecting a phone call or climbing in the shower. Which, in a way, I suppose it was to him, being interrupted.

"Does he get wet?"

"Only when he chases the animals who come to drink."

"But don't they come at twilight? Deer and raccoons?"

"Maybe." He stuffed his hands into his brown cord pockets. As the land began to slope toward a line of cypress trees, he said, "He takes his time."

"Gets that from his master."

"Don't bug me. Don't pick up on everything I say." He stopped and turned to me, close enough that our sleeves brushed. Dropping my eyes, I remembered the last time we were together, on the gravel shoulder in the drizzling rain. If he wanted me here in this rough hot field, that would be fine.

Instead, he pointed behind me. "Here he comes. Here, boy. Don't jump. Come here."

The large, tail-wagging, black Labrador obeyed all commands, greeted the stranger politely by sniffing my hands and feet and crotch, then rubbed happily against his master. He had yellow pollen on his nose and cow dung on his back feet.

The writer pointed toward a shadowed spot below the cliff, past the row of lush trees. "Down there's the swimming hole."

"Can we?" It could not be an intrusion into his villagers' misery to swim past the cottonmouth moccasins in dappled shade with a paddling dog beside us. It could not be inhabiting his space to skinny-dip, and then sun on the rocks like any native animal.

"I need to work." He turned back.

In the sun the three of us trooped back to the house.

Stopping on the long porch, Albrech gestured toward my car. "Now you've seen all there is to see—" he said.

"I want to come back inside. I don't want to be dismissed out here like a door-to-door salesman."

"If you came to see the bed, it hasn't been made in three weeks." He made the words hard.

My face flushed as if it had been slapped. "No need for that. You've already seen the bathing-suit line; and I've crawled across your brother's string."

"—Come in, then."

We re-entered the cool, thick-walled interior with its air of nineteen-thirties hard times. His written words lay in inverted stacks; his unspoken ones loomed higher still.

Standing by the poems, threats to extinguish self, I finally said what I had come for. Having made it to the place where he lived, I did not want to be ushered to the door without a confrontation. "You did not have to lie, Billy Wayne. It would have been all the same to me if you had said at once you were a home-grown boy, another Kraut among the rest who pound the pavement and listen to my show."

"I had heard it. That's why I agreed to be interviewed."

I would not be sidetracked. "I didn't have to think you had been up there grading papers and deflating poets at Bread Loaf. You could have taken responsibility for the local mess like the rest of us."

"I put a lot of stuff behind me when I came out here to the ranch. When you asked those questions, about my real name and all, it seemed simpler to go along with what you thought than to get into all of it."

"And then I obediently tagged along as a bit player to your ethnic festivals."

"You didn't have to."

"I did though. I went along with all of it. The whole production. With your presenting yourself in the oldest show on earth: now you see the slimy frog in his slick green suit, puckered up under the rose bush by the lily pond begging for a kiss. One smack he says and I'll turn into the real thing. And then, presto, there he is in his purple prince suit, with ruffles at the sleeves and silky socks. Kiss me, baby, it's all me, he says, lying all the while. Because he's only the son of the goddamn rose gardener. Well, I'm not what you think. I'm not just any blonde with frizzy hair waiting for some bandy-legged rider to trudge into view. I'm named for a grocery store, and it reserves the right to refuse service to frauds."

I reached on the mantel for the cup of tepid acrid coffee and smashed it against the stone hearth.

"There was no need for that." Slowly, painfully, the writer pushed the pieces of pottery into the winter's cold ashes. "Come sit down." He sank onto the sagging couch which was draped with a tattered chenille bedspread.

"You smell like a lily pad."

Placing his elbows on his knees, he leaned forward in his typing position, the way one sat to spin tales. "I hadn't figured out how to tell you what I was doing, or rather what I had just been doing, without getting into a lot of things I preferred to forget. One reason I stayed away from you was that it got harder to keep up the act, to go through that stuff about Connecticut, or whatever. It seemed better to forget about it, you, for the time being, until I did my stretch here, and had the book underway. Then I figured I had time to see exactly where I was."

"Didn't your family give you a hard time about this Gruene Albrech stuff? Didn't they think you had gone mad?"

"My brother is out of state. That's all the family I have." He stared at the floor. "Rather, all I claim." He indicated the couch again. "Can you sit down?"

"You think I'm here to rend your space and breathe your air."

"I thought my life depended on being sure you didn't."

I sat beside him then and put my hand on his worn brown leg. "Are those serious, then?" I pointed to the tacked-up scraps fluttering above the mantel.

"That's hard to say. They may be fair warning, as they were for some of the ones who wrote them. My idea was to give the book a try first, and then see."

"Warning to who?"

"To myself." He took my hand in his and held onto it for dear life. "I almost got up and left by the back door when your car turned in the drive."

"You heard me on the porch, but you didn't answer."

"What was there to say? You knew I was here. The Ford was out there."

"You could have said, 'Come in.'"

"You know I didn't want you to."

Which brought us to the crux of the matter. I let go his hand, the better to explain it. "But I did; I have. I opened your door and came in your room. I kissed you by the pond, Billy, and the rules of the game are you have to turn."

He bent down to retrieve a piece of the broken cup. "Turning costs too much." He tossed it into the mound of dusty ashes.

"But what choice do you have? Out here alone with the wagging, licking dog, your only options are the suicides and the Italian in your head."

"Sometimes you need to pull in until things get easier to take. Sometimes I felt even risking what we had required too much."

He pulled me down against his chest and wrapped his arms around me, holding me so I could feel his heart but so I could not read his face.

"I want to hear about it."

"You may not like what you find."

"Knowing it, whatever it is, is better than not knowing it."

"More or less what I have decided." He buried his mouth on the back of my neck. "Last summer my dad beat my mom to death. That's the lead sentence."

"Very bad." My voice was muffled by his shirt, and shock.

"When it happened I left the paper and moved my woman out. I couldn't touch her. In fact, I hadn't been with anyone until you. I thought I was going to have to drink a bottle of gin that first time, at your place."

"And I brought up the past, at once, talking about running around without my shirt in Kentucky."

"I brought it up, too. Which didn't help."

"You sleeping with your brother."

"I guess he was on my mind. He's gone wild since it happened; stays stoned all the time."

I sat up, a distance from him, the better to see the images behind his hazel eyes.

"Mom lived in terror of my dad. I could never understand it. We thought she was scared of her own shadow. We never saw him touch her. He would take after my brother and me with his belt at the least provocation—if we'd left a mess in the garage or our bikes out on the street. But he never laid a hand on her that we saw. Last year I decided to move to Dallas. Time to write about the Metroplex; investigate sloth and corruption in another city. Mostly to get out of where I was.

"As I hadn't lived with my folks since high school, I didn't think it would matter, my leaving town. I hardly saw them anyway; we had all gone our separate ways after I left home. But Mom had a fit over my leaving. She cried on the phone for an hour, 'Don't leave, Billy, please don't, he'll take it out on me.' 'Oh, come on, Mom,' I told her, 'Dad couldn't care less. Whenever I come by he's up to his ears in beer, watching the tube. He'd forget which son I am if you didn't prompt him.' I couldn't get her to get ahold of herself. Finally, I hung up. Figuring it was actually her that didn't want to let go. Patting myself on the back for cutting the apron strings.

"Apparently he had beat her for years, where it didn't show, on the back, the shoulders, the hips, the breasts. He used to pinch her until . . . So the doctor who found her told me. Dad had done just what she feared, gone after her, in such a rage that the last one of us was gone that he didn't stop in time. The doctor said he got her in the heart and kidneys both. They put heart attack on the death certificate. The doctor went home and got very drunk."

"What did you do?"

"I told you. Left. Everything. Called in flayed to the paper in Dallas and told them I wasn't coming."

"Became Gruene the writer, down from New England."

"Tried to."

"Moved in with your grandfather."

"Tried to."

"I didn't know." I looked at him with a bad pain inside, an echo of his own.

"Your fixation with graveyards drove me nuts." He made a faint smile.

"I didn't understand. For me cemeteries are the one place where there are no ambiguities—"

"—if you mean everyone is dead."

"I mean everyone is named and placed. They have given up the ghost of all those feuds and shams and accusations that go with living."

"When we went to trace the Wends and you came out of all those tombstones with that daisy chain around your neck, it reminded me of the way flowers grow out of graves."

"You kissed me for it."

"That wasn't the only reason." He did so again, very tight and hard, to demonstrate that you can want the feel of someone a lot, no matter what is on your mind.

"How could you bear that, Bill? About your mother?"

"The world is enough to put your eyes out. As I said."

It was true his bed had not been made in three weeks, or the sheets changed either. At the foot was an army blanket threaded with dog hairs. The pillow was without a case, and darkened by old coffee stains.

"No gin," he said. And then, "No petticoat."

"No mayor," I answered. "No shopkeeper."

"Nothing but the thing itself, all right?"

"The dog is welcome," I said as I pulled off my white shirt and lay my head on the matted blanket.

"I have a shoe for under your head," he said, beginning to make love to me.

At twilight we sat on the porch having a beer as the day cooled into evening.

"We can't be immigrants forever, Billy. Sooner or later we have to settle."

"Where?"

"Not here, at your borrowed ranch. Not under my rented lagustrum. I don't know. Sometimes to make it work it takes a town where the river flows green and the camera can keep its eye on the printing press. Sometimes it takes a window box with pansies."

"Are you sure it's me you want? I may not be who you think I am."

"As sure as I'll ever be."

He turned so I could look into his transparent face. "It may be peanut butter and tap water."

"That was good enough before."

"Can we count on that?"

"It's as good a place as any to begin."

SHELBY HEARON lives fifteen miles west of Austin in the Texas hill country, in a stone farmhouse on two acres of live oak and cedar, with four cats, grazing deer, and occasional visits from her two college children.